Strategic Vulnerability: New & Lengthened 2016 Anniversary Edition (Immortal Ops)

By

Mandy M. Roth

D1475358

Mandy M. Roth, Online

Mandy loves hearing from readers and can be found interacting on social media.

(copy & paste links into your browser window)

Website: http://www.MandyRoth.com

Blog: http://www.MandyRoth.com/blog

Facebook: http://www.facebook.com/ AuthorMandyRoth

Twitter: @MandyMRoth

Book Release Newsletter: mandyroth.com/ newsletter.htm

(Newsletters: I do not share emails and only send newsletters when there is a new

Mandy M. Roth

release/contest/or sales)

Strategic Vulnerability
Paranormal Shifter Military Special Ops Romance

Held prisoner in a remote testing facility in the middle of the Brazilian rain forest, subjected to torture and abuse, shape-shifter and alpha male Wilson Rousseau has long since given up hope of being rescued. Days blend together until he can't help but long for death. Saved from his isolated hell by a female's distress call, he feels an instant connection to her.

Kimberly thought she was taking a trip to South America to study indigenous plant life. She had no idea she was playing into the hands of a madman whose goal is to create a genetically altered army of super-soldiers. When she finds herself locked in a cell with Wilson, a man who would give his life to save hers, there is an instant attraction. But the dark secrets surrounding their imprisonment may change their lives forever. Can they find a way to beat the odds and be together, or will the madman win?

Dedication and Note from the Author

To the fans of the Immortal Ops Series, thank you for your continued dedication and for your love of the I-Ops. I can't believe it's been *well* over a decade since Immortal Ops book one was first published (2004) and even longer since it was first written. I will forever be thankful to my father, for instilling in me a love of science fiction; to my grandfather, for giving me such a love of history that I found myself fascinated with what the world would have been like if events had ended differently — or maybe didn't end at all (hint, hint) — to my mother, who has always told me to dream big; to my brother, who was the first victim (big grin) of listening to me tell tales; to my husband, for telling me to keep going, not to give up even when it seemed like the best choice; to my sons, who have brought me so much happiness (and a new appreciation for stain removal tips and tricks, not to mention making me quite the skilled cut and scrape fixer); and last but not least, to everyone who has fallen in love with my characters and encouraged me to keep writing. I can't thank you all enough for your support. In addition, I'd like everyone to remember the men and women in the Armed Services who are, at this very moment, putting their lives on the line for our freedom.

A note from the author about the expanded editions and what inspired The Immortal Ops:

Many things combined to create the perfect storm, if you will, for how I came up with the series idea well over a decade ago. Having been heavy into marketing and advertising and then suddenly finding myself needing to stay home to care for my boys, one of whom had additional needs, I was left craving a creative outlet.

I first tried to get my "fix" by playing video games after the boys were asleep at night. I was online and playing the first day Xbox Live launched (November 2002). I found myself getting very into first-person-shooters and military games. The more I got into playing video games, the more I wanted to read about the actual history behind the games. I found myself talking with friends who had served our country. I would devour anything they wanted to offer, listening, completely swept up in it all. Each story shared a common theme — a strong sense of brotherhood.

This appealed to me and in a relatively short period of time, I decided to do something about it. That impulse, combined with my love of history, science fiction, paranormal, and technology, as well as my love of things that go bump in the night, really was a recipe for the Immortal Ops Series to be born from my imagination. From a very early age, I've been fascinated with the supernatural, myths and legends. I have always read books that revolve around the supernatural. I cut my teeth on Stephen King, Clive Barker, Anne Rice, and the classics. Two books that made a huge impression on me were *The Island of Dr. Moreau* and of course *Dracula*.

The more I found myself digging into the history of the military and of world wars, the more I kept getting this thought in the back of my brain, pushing me forward. Urging me to combine both loves—supernatural and history. I thought, what would happen if I took a team of men who were in the military, and they were a paramilitary group, a black ops type of thing, and I combined them with my love of the paranormal?

The scary part about the Ops series is that it was born from events that actually happened in history, just with a large fictional spin put on it. I asked myself, what if I took from history, from eugenics, which so many assume started in Nazi Germany, and threaded it into the very fabric of the military team? What if I were to take a page from history and the horrible cross-breeding attempts made by Ilya Ivanov and the Nazis to create super-soldiers, who were ape and human hybrids? And what if I were to weave in even more aspects, like cloning, additional genetic engineering, and so on? What if I went a step beyond and brought in other parts of history that revolve around attempts at making super-soldiers or controlling the minds of humans?

What would happen?

What would you be left with? How damaged would the men be? What kind of government would do this? What if I were to build off the history of it all, have it where America made super-soldiers behind the scenes, and then drew back and wanted to cut ties and stop everything when Nazi Germany rose and the backlash from that hit, but, in reality, they didn't stop? And with scientific advances, how would that work? What would it look like? The answer seemed simple to me. Take all these questions to what I felt was their logical conclusion and to also blend in what I love—werecreatures and vampires.

So the idea to have shape-shifting military men who were created by the government was born. And that was how I came up with The Immortal Ops Series. I started writing in early 2000, thoughts, ideas, very short stories and then full novels and novellas. The Ops were among the first things I put together and it wasn't long after that I was published (early 2004). My then-publisher asked me if I could write something that was third-person point of view, instead of first-person, which I had first been published in. Since I had the Ops already started and the series all mapped out, it was just a matter of getting it to work as a third-person book, rather than first. Honestly, I wasn't sure I could. I'd mapped the series originally to be first-person. It took some elbow grease, but in the end it worked and the first four books were published. Reader support for them has been amazing.

Sadly, I found I had to cut a lot to make the book fit with word count restrictions then, but I'm happy to report that I have the rights back, and the first four books are being re-released with their original content.

Thank you,
Mandy M. Roth

Praise for Mandy M. Roth's Immortal Ops World

Silver Star Award—*I feel Immortal Ops deserves a Silver Star Award as this book was so flawlessly written with elements of intrigue, suspense and some scorching hot scenes*—Aggie Tsirikas—Just Erotic Romance Reviews

5 Stars—*Immortal Ops is a fascinating short story. The characters just seem to jump out at you. Ms. Roth wrote the main and secondary characters with such depth of emotions and heartfelt compassion I found myself really caring for them*—Susan Holly—Just Erotic Romance Reviews

Immortal Ops packs the action of a Hollywood thriller with the smoldering heat that readers can expect from Ms. Roth. Put it on your hot list…and keep it there! —The Road to Romance

5 Stars—*Her characters are so realistic, I find myself wondering about the fine line between fact and fiction…This was one captivating tale that I did not want to end. Just the right touch of humor*

endeared these characters to me even more— eCataRomance Reviews

5 Steamy Cups of Coffee—*Combining the world of secret government operations with mythical creatures as if they were an everyday thing, she (Ms. Roth) then has the audacity to make you actually believe it and wonder if there could be some truth to it. I know I did. Nora Roberts once told me that there are some people who are good writers and some who are good storytellers, but the best is a combination of both and I believe Ms. Roth is just that. Mandy Roth never fails to surpass herself—* coffeetimeromance

Mandy Roth kicks ass in this story— inthelibraryreview

Immortal Ops Series Helper

(This will be updated in each upcoming book as new characters are introduced.)

Immortal Ops (I-Ops) Team Members

Lukian Vlakhusha: Alpha-Dog-One. Team captain, werewolf, King of the Lycans. Book: Immortal Ops (Immortal Ops)

Geoffroi (Roi) Majors: Alpha-Dog-Two. Second in command, werewolf, blood-bound brother to Lukian. Book: Critical Intelligence (Immortal Ops)

Doctor Thaddeus Green: Bravo-Dog-One. Scientist, tech guru, werepanther. Book: Radar Deception (Immortal Ops)

Jonathon (Jon) Reynell: Bravo-Dog-Two. Sniper, weretiger. Book: Separation Zone (Immortal Ops)

Wilson Rousseau: Bravo-Dog-Three. Resident smart-ass, wererat. Book: Strategic Vulnerability (Immortal Ops)

Eadan Daly: Alpha-Dog-Three. PSI-Op and handler on loan to the I-Ops to round out the team, Fae. Book: Tactical Magik (Immortal Ops)

Colonel Asher Brooks: Chief of Operations and point person for the Immortal Ops Team. Book: Administrative Control (Immortal Ops)

Chapter One

Rain forest, South America

Kim Dunaid pushed through the dense jungle vines. They cut at her skin, digging deep in some places and breaking open cuts she'd sustained only the morning before—cuts she would have normally been able to heal over already if she were alone. She had to be away from the prying eyes of others. A branch shot back and caught her cheek. The sting told her it too had drawn blood.

The tour guide in front of her paused and glanced back at her, having the decency to appear apologetic, as he'd been the one to lose hold of the branch to begin with. She gave a tiny wave indicating she would be fine and wondered if the man was qualified to be leading the way. He'd told her the day before that the trails they'd be taking today were relatively clear.

Guess we have different views on clear paths, she thought as she glanced down at the shallow lacerations covering her hands and forearms. They would heal over relatively quickly, within a day or two without her drawing upon any of the gifts she'd been born with, but that wasn't the point.

Face it. You just might not be cut out for a life of this.

She was just happy the other guide had stopped talking. He'd been spinning tall tales of lions and other assorted animals such as polar bears that, according to him, roamed the rain forests near their current area. Some of the group of tourists that were also being led deeper and deeper into the wilds had looked frightened by the news of lions in the area. Kim just rolled her eyes at the guide's antics, knowing he was full of bologna.

She trudged along, wishing she'd brought more bug spray. So far she was averaging a bite a minute. At least it felt that way. A prickly vine dug into her lower leg, and she was thankful she was in long pants. Brad Durant, one of the other students on the trip, and someone she'd label a friend, had suggested she put the bottoms of her pant legs into the tops of her socks. He'd also advised her to avoid wearing shorts again. Wisely, she'd listened. He and his best friend Vic seemed like they'd been in a similar situation before and had come out of the other side experts.

When Professor Gisbert Krauss, had asked her, along with several other students, to go on a trip to South America for a few weeks, she'd thought it was the opportunity of a lifetime. She wasn't so sure now. They were there to study plants native to the area. Kim had an interest in studies reporting amazing results with the fungi in soil and leaf litter samples. She also had a curiosity about the antibacterial qualities associated with several of the plant extracts she'd recently began studying. The news of the finds was making its way through the scientific community, not quite at the rate she'd like, but moving all the same. It wasn't something that fascinated most people, but Kim enjoyed the work. She'd also enjoyed the chance to study in the Brazilian rain forest, or at least she had until recently.

The trip had started out fine but had become progressively odder from there on. Professor Krauss wasn't acting like himself. Back at the university he seemed even-tempered and basically boring. All in all, a nice man. Now, in the wilds of the jungle, he was agitated, and virtually impossible to talk to. Brad and Vic had noticed the change in the professor's demeanor as well. The three of them had spent the prior evening discussing the dramatic change in their professor's demeanor, unsure what had prompted the sudden personality shift.

It was probably stress and the heat. As Kim swatted at another bug, she had to wonder if she wasn't edgier than normal as well. Between the humidity and the insects, she found herself losing some of the joy she'd had about getting to study plants in the rain forest.

"Ten-minute break," yelled the very guide Kim wished would stay silent.

Kim withdrew her water bottle and took a sip, the heat turning her stomach. She wasn't hungry, and she hadn't had much in the way of an appetite since she'd arrived. The humidity and oppressive heat were partly to blame. Being unable to let her gifts free and stop masking who and what she was also contributed to her loss of appetite. Had she given in to what was natural for her, she'd have felt better than she had in years—especially being surround by so much nature, far from cities and pollution. Her kind—Fae—liked nature and thrived in it.

Pretending to be an ordinary, everyday human often sucked.

Krauss walked past, grumbling about the slow progress the group was making and how they'd never make it on time. She wasn't sure what the rush was. The plants weren't going anywhere and they had plenty of daylight left to burn.

Already today the professor had snapped at the guides and even turned his temper on the students—specifically Brad and Vic. Kim wasn't extremely close to any of her classmates because of her condition, but she didn't like seeing them berated. Vic and Brad were the two classmates she'd dare to label friends, but even that was weaker than she'd have liked. The trip to South America had them spending more time together than they had in the time she'd known them.

Brad had been the student Krauss had

focused his foul mood on the most throughout the day. Brad took it in stride, but the act still bothered Kim. Krauss had been a mentor to her at the university, and it was disheartening to watch his metamorphosis.

Something was certainly off.

Kim swatted a bug on her neck and inwardly cursed about how edible she seemed to be to insects of late. She was an all-you-can-eat buffet, traipsing around, sweaty, and barely covered.

Standing near the roots of a kapok tree, Kim slapped away yet another bug before admiring the sheer size of the tree. A grown man could lie on the ground, stretching his arms and legs as far as he could, and still not come close to the width of the trunk. It didn't matter how many kapoks they passed on their expedition, each one amazed her.

Vic walked up beside her and tapped her arm lightly. "Here."

He held a bottle of bug spray out to her. His sandy-blond hair flopped over into his green eyes and his lips twitched as if he was trying not to laugh at her. "You're going to be miserable later."

"Thank you. You're always so prepared. I should have had you teach me to pack a backpack for hiking down here. You seem to have managed to fit everything needed in yours." She returned his slightly flirtatious look with one of her own, before glancing at his pack that was now leaning against his leg. Her time with Vic at the university had taught her he was a flirt by nature and harmless— though she strongly suspected he was hiding an inner badass. She sprayed herself and as she went to return the bottle to him, she found Vic watching her with a curious look on his handsome face.

"I *so* have bug guts smeared on my forehead right now, don't I?" she asked.

Vic simply stared at her. "No. You're perfect."

"Uh, thanks," she said, placing the bottle in his hand. The spray was supposed to have a fresh, clean scent. She begged to differ with the manufacturers.

Vic shook his head and pressed the bottle against her, his hand over hers. "Nah, hang onto it. I'll get it back from you later tonight." He grinned. "Besides, I kind of think the bugs only have a taste for you."

"It's because I'm so sweet," she said, before snorting at her own lameness.

Vic let out a soft laugh as he stared around. "Kim?"

"Yes?" The strongest feeling of danger rushed over her, nearly taking her to her knees. While she was masking what she was and suppressing her inborn gifts as much as she could, they were present enough to warn her that something bad was about to happen.

Vic touched her arm and then squeezed, moving his body in front of hers in a protective manner. "Something is wrong, Kim."

She sensed it too. Vic pulled her close to him and turned in a slow circle before letting her go and motioning for her to stay put. She wasn't keen on being left alone but nodded all the same. She glanced around, trying to figure out what had caused her inner alarms to go off.

The telltale sounds of the rain forest came to a grinding halt. It was a noisy place with all the birds, insects, and animals. To have sudden silence wasn't natural. The tension in the air carried with it the threat of danger. At first, she assumed a larger predator was near them, stalking them. It wouldn't have been the first time on their expedition that they had found themselves near a large animal. While there were no lions or polar bears, there were other large predators.

There was a loud thud followed by a groan from somewhere behind her. She spun around and found Professor Krauss watching an area off to their right. It took a moment for Kim to register what she was seeing, but when she came to her senses, a scream tore free from her. Vic was there, facedown on the ground, a dart sticking out of his upper left shoulder.

"Ohmygod, Professor Krauss, Vic is hurt!" Looking to her left, she gasped, her entire body went rigid as she found Brad lying on the ground, in the direction of a stream not far from them. He too was unconscious. "So is Brad!"

Kim turned and yet another from the expedition had fallen. Confused, she snapped her gaze to the professor. For a split second, it appeared as if Krauss was smiling. Something sharp pinched her neck and she swatted at it, assuming it was another damn bug.

Coming away with a tiny dart, Kim shook her head as her body began to feel heavy. Her vision blurred and she staggered. She reached out for the professor, screaming once more as blackness swallowed her whole.

Chapter Two

Wilson Rousseau lifted his head, and pain radiated throughout his body. His vision blurred, and for a moment he could have sworn he heard the cry of a female. One who needed help—one who needed him.

A distant, yet constant, low-grade sound emitted from something his captors liked to refer to as the "scrambler." Wilson knew enough about the guy running the show, Gisbert Krauss—an insane scientist with plans to create a master race of supernaturals—to know the device was more than effective. His guess was, it was built to prevent other supernaturals from sensing the presence of one another. If his hunch was right, it was some sort of modified L.R.A.D.—long-range acoustical device.

In short, it blocked his ability to mentally or electronically call out to the Immortal Ops (I-Ops), and the rest of the I-Ops' ability to call in. If his team was even still looking for him, which he was fast beginning to doubt. But if they were, static or silence would be all that greeted them.

Again, Wilson sensed the call of a woman in need of him, even when he shouldn't have been able to receive any form of mental links with the scrambler in place. Every sore, battered, and bruised ounce of him came alive with the need to go to the woman calling for help and to protect her. He struggled against the silver-coated chains digging into his wrists and ankles. He was a shifter male, and shifters had a serious allergy to silver.

While a recent mishap—or as he preferred to refer to it, a kiss from his friend's wife—had given him a slight resistance to silver, it wasn't enough to stop the effects of prolonged exposure. Melanie, the woman who had kissed him, had shared her Fae blood with him willingly. That meant she'd passed on a few Fae traits. Without what she'd done for him, the silver-coated chains would have cut through his limbs already. The chains still would if he dared to continue to push. Understanding that fact, Wilson still tugged, needing to get to the woman he sensed was in need of him.

He couldn't have stopped himself even if he wanted. The inborn need to help the female was that great.

As quickly as the call for help from the mysterious woman had come, it faded away. It was then Wilson realized he was more than likely hallucinating as a result of the injections he'd been given and the tests they'd done on him to date. Whatever his captors had injected him with dulled his senses, making his vision blur and his body weak.

At random times, he could feel the Fae power Melanie had passed on to him trying to surface, but the magik either wasn't sure what to do or knew he was clueless, so it didn't bother lending a hand. It probably figured he'd kill himself attempting to wield it. At this rate, he'd rather be dead than living like he was, so he was open to the idea.

Groaning, he moved his head around, trying to alleviate the kinks from his upper shoulders and neck. It didn't work. Beyond that, his throat was dry and his body was weak. The food wasn't fit for human consumption. Maggots infested the majority of it, and the rest was in a state of decomposition. After a certain point, Wilson had forced some of the food down only to find it coming back up quickly. Still, any nourishment he could get was needed if he planned on regaining his strength and escaping.

And he fully intended to escape.

In shifted form, Wilson wasn't too particular about what he ate or drank—that being said, his rat form wouldn't even eat the food his captors continued to try to pawn off on him. Considering his rat form tended to eat just about anything, that was saying a lot as to how dire his situation was.

He tipped his head back, giving in to the need to sleep. He was almost completely out when a scent like he'd never smelled before came to him, causing his cock to harden and his body to ignite with need. He looked up to find Krauss's men dragging an unconscious woman past his cell.

The fierce need to protect her overtook him. Wilson surged forth, yanking with all his might against his restraints, reaching for the woman. He knew then it had been her call for help that he'd tried to answer. She hadn't been a figment of his imagination or the result of drugs. She was real and she needed him.

"Get away from her!" Wilson roared, his body protesting his every movement, pain lancing through his extremities.

The men stalled and stared at him before sharing a curious look.

"*He'll* want to hear about this," one said.

The other nodded. "Definitely."

They continued down the hall, dragging the unconscious woman behind them. Wilson thrashed against his restraints, trying to get free, until the pain was so unbearable that he passed out cold.

Chapter Three

"Other than being hot," a deep voice said, pulling Kim from her sleep, "this one is useless. The boss swears she's got supernatural blood in her, but she didn't put up any fight or show signs of being anything but a sexy piece of ass."

Kim blinked. Her head felt heavy and her vision was somewhat fuzzy. She tried to sit up, but found she couldn't. Panic hit as she understood she was strapped down to a bed of sorts. Tugging, she tried in vain to break free from her restraints. The urge to cry out for help was great, but she knew better. If help was close, she wouldn't have been strapped to a bed, and letting whoever was talking know she was awake seemed less than wise.

Glancing around, she spotted bars and her stomach dropped. She was in a cell. Still managing to maintain her composure, Kim looked in the direction the voice had come from but couldn't see anyone there.

"I agree," another male voice said. "But the boss was right. She is a prize for breeding."

Who were they talking about? Prize for breeding? This wasn't happening. She had to be dreaming. Had she hit her head? Was she lying on the rain forest floor right this very minute? She drew in a sharp breath.

"*Shh.*"

Kim's blood ran cold at the sound of the deep voice. She lay perfectly still, praying whoever was close to her wouldn't realize she was awake.

"I'm not with them. And I'd never hurt you," the man whispered. "Are you in a lot of pain?"

Something deep within Kim told her to trust the man, whoever he was. Swallowing hard, she turned to face his direction and was shocked to see how close a pair of chocolate-brown eyes were. She'd expected the man to be in an adjacent cell. He wasn't. He was next to her, shackled to the wall. His squared jaw was covered with a beard. Red, brown, and even blond showed in it. His hair hung just past his ears and was brown with hints of golden blond running through it. The man, even in his obvious state of disarray, was gorgeous.

The tan t-shirt he wore was ripped and bloody, as were his pants. It was easy to see he'd been beaten a multitude of times. The rather angry-looking gash on his upper right cheek made her chest tight. Kim bit her lower lip, no longer worried about herself, but rather concerned greatly for the man locked in the cell with her. "You're hurt."

A soft nervous chuckle came from him. "I'm fine. Though I've been sitting here worried sick about you. I wasn't sure you'd ever wake up." He lifted his bound hands. "And I couldn't get to you. I'm so sorry." His forehead creased. "Do you know where you are?"

"No." She sighed, being sure to keep her voice barely above a whisper. The horrible stench of the cell made her stomach tight, and the weight of the ordeal began to press in on her. Kim took a soothing breath, willing herself not to panic. She thought back to the events leading up to this point. "The last thing I remember was talking to Vic about the bugs down here and then Professor Krauss calling my name." She looked around the dark, dank cell. "Then I woke up here. Why am I strapped down?"

The man let out a low growl, sounding very much like an animal. His eyes widened with revulsion. "You were with Krauss on purpose?"

"Yes. Why? Is he hurt?" Thoughts of Professor Krauss being dead filled her. Alarm for the rest of the group members washed over her. She'd seen Vic and Brad both lying on the ground, neither moving. "Oh gods, all the others. Were they hurt too?"

"Others?"

She blinked back tears, refusing to give in to them so soon. "I came on the trip with several other grad students." She thumped her head against the cot, unable to understand how it was she came to be strapped to it to begin with. "Krauss was excited about bringing us down to study the native plants. This wasn't supposed to happen. This was just —"

"Study plants?" the man asked, jerking on his chains. "You mean you're not in league with Krauss and his experiments on humans?"

Shocked, Kim stared out from wide eyes. "Experiments on humans? What are you talking about?" She glanced at the straps binding her down. Tears tried again to surface but she fought them back. "W-what did they do to me?"

"What's your name?" he asked, clearly trying to change the subject. She knew enough to let him.

"Kimberly, *erm*, Kim."

"Well, Kim, I'm Wilson Rousseau, your new roommate." He glanced around the cell before resting his head against the stone wall. Pieces of his shaggy hair fell into his eyes, and he blew them out. "It's not the Ritz, that's for sure. I'd lie and say you get used to it, but I don't think you'd fall for that. Plus the room service here sucks major ass."

The nervous energy building in Kim left her laughing softly at Wilson's attempt at humor. "No. I wouldn't fall for that. Have you tried talking to the manager? Maybe a complaint or two would get him to act on it."

Wilson's eyes crinkled in amusement. "I did try discussing the matter with him." He pulled on the chains and winked. "This was his answer to it. Great customer service, huh? I'm planning to leave a scathing review online later."

Another nervous chuckle escaped her. She lifted her head as much as she could while strapped and stared around. The bars appeared to be iron and they looked thick. Rusted spots could be seen in two of the corners, and she wondered how strong those points were. She tried to free her natural-born gifts, but nothing happened. Panic assailed her, and she realized that whatever she'd been given had somehow managed to block her ability to wield magik, at least for now.

Humidity coated the already stale air, practically choking her as she took a deep breath in. Kim swallowed hard, refusing to break down. She couldn't. Not yet. Yes, this was beyond scary. Hell, it was terrifying, but admitting defeat so soon wasn't an option. She was stronger than that.

Kim glanced at Wilson. The very sight of him seemed to ease her nerves. "How long have we been here?"

He squirmed, looking as if he were trying to scratch an itch on his upper left shoulder blade. "Ah, that's a good question. I think I've been here about two and a half months, maybe three, but I'm not sure. Could be longer or not. Everything has pretty much run together for me. They had me pretty doped up for a while so your guess is as good as mine. I do know that you've been here for a little over two weeks."

"Two weeks?" She couldn't believe what she'd heard. There was no way she'd been there for two weeks.

"Kim, they went out of their way to keep you sedated and lying flat. I don't know why for sure, but I've got my suspicions." He rubbed his temple, the shackle on his wrist keeping him from being too productive though. The action was more a light swipe than anything. "They wheel you out of here several times a day, talking about needing to monitor your progress."

"My progress?" She tried to sit up and failed. As she stared down at herself, Kim realized that, unlike Wilson, she wasn't dressed in street clothes. She had on a hospital gown. "What the...? Where are my clothes? Ohmygod, did they...?" Unable to bring herself to ask if they'd raped her, Kim locked gazes with Wilson. "Wil?"

Sorrow filled his chocolate brown eyes. "I honestly don't know. These people are crazy. They believe they can genetically alter anything. I don't think they did, *uhh,* but they didn't stop pumping me full of drugs until after you'd been here for a couple of days. I'm going to kill every last one of them for daring to harm you."

The man's words floated back to her. "Prize for breeding... Ohmygod, Wil." The tears she'd so desperately tried to hold in let loose.

"Look who is up, Doc," a deep voice said from the other direction. "Aww, what's a matter, sweetheart? Don't like the company we gave you?"

She blinked back her tears and glared at the brute who stood on the outside of the cell. His shaved head and thick, blond goatee added to his already sinister look. His beady blue eyes landed on her as his lip curled. "Mmm, you are even sexier than I thought. You've got the greenest eyes I've ever seen. Must be from the faerie in your blood. I'm betting that's where you get that tight fucking body from too." The man blatantly adjusted his cock through his pants. "I was under the impression that all Fae were blonde with blue eyes. How did you manage to get black hair and green eyes, cupcake?"

"Fae?" she echoed, shocked to hear the word mentioned so casually when it had been instilled in her since birth never to repeat it. Humans were not to know of the Fae. The rules laid out to her had been simple. "What are you talking about? Faeries, like in the myths? They're not real."

He scratched his goatee. "Yet I'm starin' at one right now. Not much of a myth. The hair, why isn't it blonde? You dye it black? I could look elsewhere." His gaze raked down her and centered between her legs.

She swallowed hard, not liking the hungry look in the man's eyes. "My father has black hair. I get it from him," she said, her voice low.

"He has green eyes too."

He lifted a chart and marked something in it. "Interesting. And your mother. Is she the Fae then? She got blonde hair and blue eyes?"

"I couldn't tell you about my mother because she ran off shortly after she popped me out. Now that you got the abridged version of my so-called life, can we go now?"

"We?" the man asked, arching a brow. "You're speaking for the rat now too?"

By rat, Kim guessed the man meant Wilson. She didn't back down. "I'm sure he's enjoyed his stay here as much as me, but I think he'd prefer leaving too. Not that your hospitality hasn't been *overwhelming*." It was hard to hide the sarcasm in her voice. She wanted to bounce the man's head against the bars.

"Your mouth is going to get you into trouble, bitch."

"Don't call her a bitch, asshole," Wilson bit out.

The man pulled a handgun from his waist and fired at Wilson.

Wilson jerked, hitting the wall behind him

hard enough to cause an echo. Kim screamed and fought against her restraints as blood seeped from Wilson's shoulder.

"No!" She tried to reach him but couldn't.

The bald man laughed. "Open your mouth again and I'll aim for your head. I doubt you can heal that one, dickhead."

"Mendel!" someone called out.

The bald man licked his lower lip as his gaze bore into her. "I'll be back, cupcake. I'd like to teach you some manners and find out if you're telling the truth about having black hair naturally." He rubbed his clothed cock. "Should be educational all the way around."

Kim waited until Mendel was gone before focusing on Wilson. "Ohmygod, Wil, are you…"

He winced. "I'll be fine. He likes to do that."

"You mean he's shot you before?" She took a deep breath, doing her best to soak in everything.

I'm not going to panic. I'm not going to panic.

Wilson nodded. "Daily."

"What? He shoots you every day?"

Okay, I'm going to panic.

"Kim, it's okay. I'll be fine." He moved as much as his chains permitted, trying to reach out to her. Pain washed over his face and she knew his effort to comfort her cost him greatly. "Mendel is trigger happy. I'll be okay. Promise."

"How are you alive?"

He stiffened and cleared his throat. "It's complicated."

"Complicated? Oh, that is a good one," a familiar, heavily German-accented voice said.

Chapter Four

Kim looked up to find Krauss standing just outside of the cell. "Professor, you're okay. I thought you were—" She stopped and narrowed her gaze on him. Something wasn't right. He didn't look as though he'd suffered at all. In fact, he looked damned comfy. Not to mention he was outside of the bars. As her mind wrapped around it all, anger flashed through her. "You did this. You're the reason we're here, aren't you?"

The short, chubby man winked. "So sorry, Kimberly. I needed you here. You were too career driven to ever agree to willingly allow me to run tests on you. I have to admit, I thought you were only pretending to be human. I had no idea you truly thought yourself to be one."

Confused, she shook her head, deciding it best to avoid anything pertaining to her being human or not. "What? Professor, tests? I don't understand. This trip was to study indigenous plants of the rain forest." She tugged at her restraints. "What have you done to me?"

A wicked laugh ripped free of him. "Kimberly, the moment I read your file and saw your picture, I knew you would blindly trust me. It is your nature. You are also not a violent person and in excellent health. The addition of your supernatural blood made you the perfect candidate for what we are trying to accomplish." He pulled a key from his front pocket and unlocked the cell. "You have proven to be a wise choice."

Kim lay still, unsure what Krauss would do. He approached slowly and placed his hand on her lower abdomen. A sickening grin spread over his face as he palmed her, causing Kim to shudder. He laughed. "Do I repulse you?"

Assuming it was a rhetorical question, Kim remained silent. Krauss rubbed her lower abdomen once more. "It still amazes me that you, of all the test subjects, were receptive."

Receptive? She held in the scream wanting desperately to come.

Krauss looked her over, his demeanor smarmy, different than it had been back home. This felt real. He was truly the bastard standing before her. "It was luck that you were at the height of your cycle when I brought you in. I think my choice for a match for you was excellent. Wouldn't you agree?"

"Get your filthy fucking hands off her, you piece of shit," Wilson said, not seeming to care that his last outburst had gotten him shot. Apparently, being chained in a cell had affected his common sense, that or he had very little sense to begin with. Either way, he'd end up dead if he continued.

She stared at him. "Wil, please."

Krauss's smile grew. "Interesting."

Kim didn't like the sound of that. "What did you do to me?"

"I've given you the opportunity to be the mother to the next generation of super-soldiers."

"You son of a bitch!" Wilson fought against his restraints, rattling them and growling like an animal. "I will kill you. Know that."

"I am sure you like to think as much," Krauss said nonchalantly. He took hold of the strap on Kim's ankle and undid it. Running his fat hand up her leg, he came to a stop on her inner thigh. "I am going to release you. Try not to overexert yourself, Kimberly. So far, everything is going well. I would be *very*," he squeezed her thigh hard enough to leave a bruise, "upset if anything happened to you. You're very special to our program."

For a moment, she couldn't breathe. Shaking her head, Kim stared up at Krauss, worried he'd had her raped and might have even done it himself.

A deep laugh came from him. "Oh, fear not, young one. I oversaw the procedure necessary to produce the next wave of warriors. It was sterile and done in a lab, Kimberly. I have not," he grinned, "*as of yet*, allowed a man to commit the act naturally. Though," he glanced at Wilson, "I imagine this one will take you soon enough."

The idea of Wilson pinning her to the bed and having his way with her should have terrified Kim. It didn't. It excited her. Her skin began to tingle at the very thought of Wilson touching her. Shocked, she looked toward Wilson to find him watching her closely, as if he knew she was anything but repulsed by him.

Krauss undid her other ankle, and Kim stayed as calm as she could, not wanting to tip her hand. "You're taking the news better than I thought you would." He touched her cheek lightly before moving to her wrists and undoing the straps there. "I knew in my heart you would be perfect, Kimberly. I knew I could trust you to do the right thing, to be a good girl." He helped her sit up and directed his gaze out toward the hallway. "Bring her something to wear!"

In a matter of seconds, another beefy man appeared, this one carrying a handful of clothing. He gave the clothes to Krauss who, in turn, handed them to Kim. "There is a shower in the corner. My apologies for the lack of privacy you'll have, but I'm sure you'll make do. I'll have soap brought in momentarily. Is there anything you need? Aside from being let go, of course."

She put her chin up defiantly. "Wilson needs medical attention."

Krauss laughed, unswayed by her stance. "He is fine. Besides, he does not allow our people near him when he is not sedated. Shall I have him shot with another tranquilizer? It might be best considering what we'll be injecting him with very shortly. Shall we knock him out, Kimberly?"

"No," she said a little too quickly.

"Are you sure? I like to push how far my test subjects can go, and you should know he's had an unusual interest in you since you first arrived." Krauss smiled. "In fact, the moment he saw my men dragging you in, he went crazy, trying to get to you, trying to save you from your fate."

Kim's gaze flickered to Wilson. Had he really done such a thing? The look in his brown eyes told her he had. He'd do it again. She knew it. "I don't want him knocked out. He's been through enough."

Krauss touched her knee and gave it a good squeeze. "What if I told you my men will be administering a drug that will drive him mad with lust, with need? Would you want him tranquilized then?" Krauss leaned in more. "He's chained, for now, but can you imagine what he will be like, struggling to get to you, to fuck you, to fill you so full of his seed he can't see straight?"

Yes. Therein lay the problem. Kim wanted exactly that and she shouldn't. She didn't know Wilson, but it didn't matter. She more than wanted him.

She jerked her knee away from Krauss as Wilson yanked on the chains holding him. He growled. "Sedate me! Do it now! You know goddamn well if I lose control and take her, it could kill her! You of all people know how dangerous it is to mix our semen with—"

Kim drew in a sharp breath and Krauss laughed. "Changing your mind, Kimberly? The *animal* speaks the truth. Under normal circumstances, his semen is deadly to a human. Too powerful. Too full of supernatural DNA for the human to bear, leaving them either in a state of withdrawal, which they die from, or pregnant with a child they aren't strong enough to see to term." He reached for her lower abdomen. "But you're different, Kimberly. You can not only tolerate what he offers, but are so receptive to it. So...*very* receptive." He licked his lower lip. "I'll leave the last bit a secret. For now. But I will offer again to have him sedated after he's injected with his daily dose of meds."

Kim stared at Wilson, doing her best to keep her emotions in check. Wilson shook his head, pleading with his eyes. "Do it, Kim. Tell him you want me—"

"I want him," she whispered, realizing after the fact that she'd slipped in what she should have said. She opened her mouth to correct herself but stopped, letting her statement stand.

Krauss looked as if he would leap for joy. "Very interesting."

"I don't want him to be shot up with anything." She reached for Krauss and stopped just short of touching him. "Please don't hurt him anymore, Professor. Please. I'll do whatever you ask me to but only if you stop hurting him."

Krauss seemed to think upon it for a bit before tipping his head. "I could have you put in the cell next to this one, separate from him. There are other females here I could bring in. Ones who volunteered for the greater good of science and ones who want nothing more than to be fucked by the animal you see behind me. I personally do not see what they do when they look at him, but these females have been tripping over themselves for a chance to be fucked by him."

Tears welled but she kept hold of them as she stared past Krauss at Wilson. "I don't see an animal. I see a man. A man who has been tortured and who has somehow kept his humanity through it all."

"Very interesting, indeed," Krauss whispered before smiling. "Then you do not look hard enough, Kimberly. For he is an animal. He could rip an unwilling partner apart with ease while fucking her. Shall I sedate him, or remove you from his clutches before the next phase of testing begins? I like you. It's why I'm giving you the choice."

She glared at him, understanding the man's game more than she wanted to. "No, you're giving me the choice because you like to push your test subjects. You said as much yourself. You want to see what I'll do to keep him safe, don't you?"

"So intelligent." He stroked her inner thigh

and she wanted to release her hidden powers and blast him away. If only she could. "So beautiful and so innocent. See where it is I am coming from, Kimberly. See it and understand it. A woman like you could spend eternity by my side, helping me raise an army."

She fought the urge to vomit.

Chapter Five

Krauss moved in close enough to kiss her. Thankfully he didn't or she would have really been sick. "Now that you're on to my reasoning behind giving you a choice, what will you do to keep him safe, Kimberly?"

"Nothing," Wilson bit out, shocking Kim because of how softly Krauss had whispered the question. Wilson shouldn't have been able to hear it, yet he had. "She'll do nothing. Get her out of my cell. I don't want her here. I want —"

She would have been hurt had she not sensed Wilson's lies.

Krauss apparently sensed the lies as well because he called Wilson's bluff. "Very well. I shall have her moved to the cell next to yours. I have two other males waiting in the wings. Their bodies are so pumped full of aphrodisiacs they can't even wear clothing—it burns. I'm sure they'll enjoy two-on-one time with Kimberly. She already knows them. Brad and Vic."

Brad and Vic? They were alive and being

held captive too?

Wilson roared to life, jerking so hard against his chains that for a moment she thought he'd break free, or at the very least, rip a chunk of the wall out. "You will not touch her! No one will!"

It made her chest tight, seeing the sheer determination to protect her in his gaze and knowing he was powerless to do so. Unable to stand another moment of it, Kim touched Krauss's shoulder and avoided the urge to retch. "I want to stay with Wilson. You said I'm valuable to you and your project. If that's true, and I think it is…" She kept back the part about sensing the truth in his words. He wouldn't let her be harmed. Not yet anyway. "I don't know what it is you're doing, or what your end goal is, but I do know I cannot and will not watch that man suffer another minute."

The sly smile that swept over Krauss's face told Kim she'd played into his hands as he'd assumed she would. If it kept Wilson safe, it didn't matter. "Such a good girl, Kimberly. So caring." He stroked her leg. "I will offer you one additional gift for your honesty."

"You'll unchain him?" she asked, hopeful.

"If you wish, but that wasn't the gift, Kimberly." He stepped back a bit. "I will have another female brought in during the height of his *attraction* — shall we say — and she will be a willing participant."

"I'm not fucking anyone or anything," Wilson said, a low growl following.

That wasn't the truth and Kim knew it. She could sense Wilson holding something back, and when she met his gaze, she knew what it was — he could and would fuck her if it came down to it. Her, but no one else. The thought should have terrified her. It didn't. It gave her the resolve she needed to lift her head high and meet Krauss's gaze.

"You bring anyone else into this mix and you will not have my cooperation. You've apparently studied me long enough to know what type of person I am." *Or at least you think you know.* "If that's the case, then you're well aware of how resourceful I can be, Professor. I see you have no respect for Wilson and limited use of him because of the way you let your men treat him. I don't get the impression you're so willing to let them do the same to me."

Something flashed in Krauss's gaze, telling Kim she was right. He wouldn't allow her to be harmed just yet.

"I want to remain with Wilson, and you will not bring in other women or men, or allow your men to continue to torture him. I want to be able to treat his wounds, help him get cleaned up, and if I'm right, he's not been fed a decent meal since he's been here. I want him to eat."

She swallowed hard, continuing on her spiel. "If you think you can sneak things into his food, know that I'll eat it first. If you don't want or need me, then by all means, administer something harmful—I'd rather be dead than here if that helps to ease your mind any."

Her gifts tapped into Krauss's paranoia, and she nearly rejoiced to know they were still there, working their way through whatever they'd done to her. Krauss needed her way more than he wanted to admit, and he needed her safe and calm. "Wilson will be unchained and left with you and *you* alone, Kimberly."

Krauss motioned to the man who had brought her clothing. "Paquin, gather what Kimberly will need. Bring her soap and," he ran his fingers through her hair, "shampoo. She has the most beautiful hair."

She shuddered, wanting desperately for him to step away from her.

"Yes, sir."

Krauss reached for her cheek and she moved off the bed quickly, scrambling toward Wilson. Krauss laughed. "So, my touch does repulse you."

She knew better than to answer that in particular. She glanced back at Wilson. "He needs clean clothes. The ones he's in are hanging on him by a thread." Kim left off the part about them smelling horrible.

Krauss chuckled. "I have always admired your resolve, Kimberly. Very well. I will also see to it that he is provided with clean clothing, but I should warn you. He is a trained killer. He could snap your neck with little effort."

"He won't hurt me."

I hope.

Kraus inclined his head. "If you say so." He turned to walk away but stopped in mid-stride. "Have fun, you two." With that, he walked away, leaving his flunky to lock the cell behind him.

The man thrust a key through the bars at her and shook his head. "I can't believe you're going to free that thing."

Kim's legs were shaky as she stood, and for a split second, she thought she'd fall. Bending down, she retrieved the key and ignored the man. She went to Wilson's side and knelt down before him. Unable to help herself, she reached to touch the gash on his cheek but stopped just short of it. "Wil?"

He closed his eyes and exhaled loudly. "I'm fine, Kim. Just another day at the office."

She went to work on his shackles and noticed how raw the skin on his wrists and ankles was. "Do I need to beg you not to snap my neck?" she asked with a wink.

"No." Wilson stretched his arms and legs, wincing slightly. "Thank you. But I should tell you that pushing Krauss isn't safe. He's a sick man, Kim."

Nodding, Kim moved a little bit closer to Wilson. "Is he gone?"

"Yeah, they're all gone now."

Her lip began to tremble as she gave in to the need to cry. Before she knew it, Wilson had his arms around her, holding her close. It wasn't like she even knew the man, yet she found comfort in his arms. At first, it was hard to ignore the fact he smelled like he'd been rolling in the city dump, but it wasn't his fault and she knew it. She also knew on some level that he needed the comfort of human touch as well. She was also sure he was safe. As she realized she was indeed cuddling with a complete stranger, Kim drew back slightly, wiping her eyes and glancing at his shoulder. No bullet hole remained. In fact, there was absolutely no sign he'd been hurt at all.

"Your shoulder…it's healed."

That wasn't possible.

He sighed and her gut clenched. Scrambling away from Wilson, Kim drew her knees to her chest. "W-what? How? Who?"

Chapter Six

"Can you sense them?" Jon Reynell asked, bent in the brush, feeling slightly naked without his normal sniper camouflage suit on. He wanted a cigarette and a drink, but that wasn't to be at the moment. It wasn't the time or the place, not that much had stopped him as of late when it came to drinking. He wasn't proud of how he'd taken to handling the passing of two of his best friends, Lance and Wilson, but he was coping the best he could. Besides, he was doing his job, going through the daily motions. What else could anyone ask for?

He stared out into the dense foliage, tapping into his supernatural vision but finding nothing out of the norm. The team captain, Lukian Vlakhusha, put a hand up and motioned for all present to stop and crouch. The remaining I-Ops—Jon, Thaddeus Green, and Geoffroi "Roi" Majors, who were only minus Eadan Daly on the mission—did as instructed.

Green, the team's doctor and scientist,

glanced at Jon and then toward Lukian. Even Green seemed slightly annoyed with their current mission. Jon still couldn't believe they'd been forced to take the jet and head to South America again, only months after they'd last been there, all because three stubborn women refused to listen to reason.

He was very happy he wasn't mated.

Women were nothing more than complications.

Jon let out a soft laugh. "Is it me or does anyone else find it funny we're doing this when all we're after is a bunch of women?"

Roi shushed him. "The women we're after are lethal. Melanie took on an entire group of enemy hostiles with one weapon and lived to tell the tale." Roi glanced at Green, who was mated to Melanie. "That's something to tell the kids when they're older... Hey, did you know Mommy can kick my ass?"

Jon tried not to laugh but failed. Roi was right. Melanie was fierce.

Shrugging, Roi motioned to Lukian. "Hell, Lukian's wife is just as bad. Peren could so take us."

Jon snorted, keeping his opinions on Roi's wife to himself. Of the three women they were trying to locate, Missy, Roi's mate, was the most dangerous. The sideways glance Roi cast in Jon's direction said he knew as much.

"I, for one, am damn relieved they're deadly. It means their chances of staying alive are all the better," Lukian said, his voice low, his words clipped. "I can't believe they took off on this fool's mission alone. When I find them I'm going to —"

Green nodded, as did Roi. Green spoke, "We're all going to wring their necks."

"What the hell possessed them to lie to us?" Roi asked, letting out a low whistle. "Wilson is dead and gone. We've lost too many men this year, and I can't believe the girls would put themselves at risk. Running through the jungle like crazed banshees won't bring Wilson back, no matter how much we all wish that were the case. It'll get someone killed and —"

"Three hormonal pregnant women should not be here period," Green said, ever the one concerned with medical conditions.

Jon kept his thoughts to himself. While he was also concerned for the welfare of the three women, he was glad someone had picked up where he'd left off. He'd spent far longer in South America when Wilson had gone missing than any other teammate. He didn't fault his brothers in arms. No. They'd done all they could to try to track down any leads on what had happened to Wilson's body, but the trail had gone cold.

Each and every one of them had struggled to make sense of what had happened several months back, when they'd been ambushed by the enemy, outside of their campgrounds.

The women refused to admit Wilson was dead, and Jon wanted to believe with all his might that they were right. If they were, it would mean his best friend was still alive. But it would also mean the I-Ops had given up prematurely on one of their own, assuming the man dead.

Closing his eyes, Jon did what he often did when he was in stressful situations—he asked for a guiding hand from a higher power and from his mother who had passed long ago.

When he opened his eyes, a nagging feeling started in the pit of his gut. He crept forward slowly, touching Roi's shoulder. "Do you sense that?"

"Sense what?" Roi asked.

Jon stared around. "I'm not sure, but it's something, or rather nothing."

Roi cocked a brow. "Short on sense with that one, Jon."

Lukian tipped his head, nodding. "He's right. Nothing. Absolutely nothing."

"Huh?" questioned Roi, appearing lost.

Green looked around. "You're right. There is nothing."

"Hello? Earth to anyone remaining who is sane?" Roi rubbed his temples. "You all would pick now to have a breakdown."

Green huffed. "What Jon is pointing out is the absence of everything we *should* be sensing, hearing, noticing."

Jon saw the realization flicker through Roi's eyes as the man huffed. "Aha."

"L.A.R.D?" Green prompted.

Lukian didn't look pleased, but he inclined his head. "That would be my guess."

"That's why none of you can communicate telepathically with your mates," Jon offered. He'd wondered why the men kept mentioning being unable to reach their women on the mental pathways the mated pairs shared.

They nodded.

"Shit," Roi said. "This just went from bad to worse."

Jon didn't want to be the first to say it, but someone had to. "If L.A.R.D. is involved, Wilson could very well be alive but unable to contact us."

Lukian glanced at him and sighed. "I want to believe too, Jon, but the odds of that are slim. You understand that, right?"

With a tiny nod, he looked out at the jungle, hope springing forth in the pit of his stomach for the first time in over two months.

*

"He's got to be close, right?" Melanie asked, taking a seat on a downed log, her ankles killing her from the swelling.

Peren sat next to her, dropping her sack

onto the ground with a thud. "You'd think. Hey, are you sure you sensed him around here and then the feeling just up and vanished?"

Missy stood near them, glancing around, ever vigilant. "I'm not picking up anything anymore, and that right there tells me we're close." She glanced at Melanie. "We'll find Wilson."

Melanie touched her stomach lightly. "But will he still be alive when we do?"

Peren tossed an arm around her. "No thinking negatively. We've come this far and done this much. I have to believe that in the end it wasn't for nothing."

Melanie sighed. "Green is going to kill me for this stunt. I just couldn't walk away and live my life under the false assumption Wilson is dead."

Peren and Missy exchanged knowing looks. It was Missy who broke the silence. "We should get moving. Before everything around us seemed to go still, I was sensing something new. My guess, our husbands. If we don't want to find ourselves being dragged back to the States kicking and screaming, we need to hustle. Wilson needs us. Let's go."

With a nod, Melanie and Peren stood, ready to continue on their quest.

Chapter Seven

Wilson rubbed his raw wrists, hoping his natural healing ability would handle those too. The chains were made of silver, and thanks to his friend's wife—Melanie— Wilson was no longer as deathly allergic to silver as he'd once been. Though it would take him longer to heal them than normal. Krauss's men had taken great joy in learning that lead did still burn him. They shot him at least once a day, and it normally took Wilson the remainder of the day to heal the wound. Bizarrely enough, the moment Kim touched him, his body flared with heat and he felt it forcing the bullet out before healing over.

The second they'd first wheeled Kim into his cell two weeks ago, his body had reacted oddly to her. Her scent, a mix of citrus and flowers, had assailed him, making his cock harden to the point it was more painful than the torture Krauss's men had taken to inflicting. He could still vividly remember staring at the long, silky, black strands of her hair as they cascaded over the side of the gurney, nearly touching the floor. Kim's creamy skin seemed flawless and her breathing was soft, barely there.

Each and every time one of Krauss's goons came in to take her away, Wilson had tried to break free and tear their heads off. The fierce need to protect her was unlike anything he'd ever before experienced. It was raw. Seeing her tuck herself away from him now, afraid of him, stung.

Reaching out, Wilson cringed as his muscles ached from lack of use. "Kim, I won't hurt you."

"You're not human," she whispered, her voice so low that his supernatural hearing almost missed it.

"No. But neither are you if you're here. Krauss has a hard-on for the paranormal. He thinks he can create a race of unstoppable super-soldiers and somehow manage to cheat death."

She seemed to think about what he'd said for a bit. Her brow furrowed. "How did you heal the bullet wound?"

Sighing, Wilson pushed to his feet. His legs

were shaky and gave out on him. As he crashed to the floor, Kim moved toward him with a speed no human possessed and did her best to ease him to his feet.

"Are you okay?"

His cock began to lengthen at an alarming rate. At six two, he wasn't the tallest I-Op, but was tall all the same. Kim's five-foot-eight frame fit nicely to him, seeming to mold against him. As her hand settled against his abs, he drew in a shaky breath. "I'm…fine."

"You don't sound fine."

Because my dick is hard enough to hammer nails. All I want to do is sink to the floor and bury myself deep in you.

Kim's green eyes widened and she lifted her hand off him quickly. For a second, Wilson thought she might have actually heard his thoughts, but that was absurd. It had taken decades for he and the other I-Ops to speak telepathically to one another. Even with them it required great effort and a close proximity. In theory, he'd be able to read his mate's thoughts and she could read his, but Kim wasn't his mate. She couldn't be.

"Umm, no offense, Wil, but I think you should shower before me." Kim laughed softly, and the sound moved through him, caressing him in places it shouldn't.

The very fact she'd shortened his name to Wil would have normally pissed him off. But hearing her utter the nickname seemed to calm him. He smiled, genuinely amused for the first time in months. "I smell that bad, huh?"

She wrinkled her nose and he couldn't help but laugh.

"I'll take that as a yes," he said. "So, how do you want me to do this?"

She bit her lower lip. "What do you mean?"

"Should I strip naked now or do you want to—"

Pink splashed over her cheeks and upper neck, driving him mad with lust. "Umm, I'll turn around." She spun around so fast that her gown opened in the back, revealing an apple-shaped ass.

Wilson bit back a moan as he grabbed hold of his clothed cock just in time to lose control and come. Humiliated, he faced the shower nozzles and turned the cold water on full blast, not caring that he was still dressed. He stood there, freezing for several minutes until his dick finally decided to play dead. It didn't help that Kim's scent clung to the air around him.

A soft, sultry giggle sounded behind him. "I was going to ask if you wanted some soap but I think my first question should be if you'd like to take your clothes off."

"Dammit," he whispered as his cock flared to life with thoughts of Kim begging him to take his clothes off for other reasons. "Uh, yeah." Peeling his wet, ripped T-shirt from his body, Wilson chucked it onto the floor next to him as he watched the dirty water run down the drain in the floor. He started to undo his pants and stopped when Kim tapped his shoulder.

"Soap." She held a bar out to him.

"I really must smell bad." He winked as he put his hand over hers to take the soap. The minute their skin touched, heat flared up his arm. Kim jerked her hand away from his, obviously feeling it too. Her emerald eyes widened a second before she backed away from him quickly. "Kim?"

"I'll wait over there and then I'll take my turn," Kim said, a nervous note to her voice.

The very idea of Kim being naked and wet near him did little to help Wilson's lust. He swallowed hard and focused on the wall. It didn't help. He pulled his pants from his body. They were now water-soaked and still full of caked dirt, blood, and things he didn't want to focus too hard on. As he bent to kick them away, his sore, unused muscles acted up. He groaned, wincing slightly.

"Here," Kim said, suddenly close enough that water was splashing her as well as him. She took the soap from him and began working up lather. She touched his back lightly at first, scrubbing away the filth they'd left him in for months. It felt good to be touched, good to be cared for and tended to, especially with what he'd endured.

Wilson stood, frozen in place, his backside facing her, unsure what to do or say. He normally had a joke for about every occasion. He seemed to lack one for this. Never did he expect to be locked in a cell with the most beautiful woman he'd ever seen and then to be standing naked under a stream of water, being washed by her.

His cock twitched to life and he jerked, trying his best to shield it from her view. He suppressed a moan as Kim moved in behind him, rubbing his back as she washed it tenderly.

Yeah, just my luck to end up in a hellhole only to have an angel show up and give me her version of a sponge bath.

Kim let out a soft laugh. "Minus the sponge, of course."

Wilson stiffened, positive he'd not said that out loud.

She moved to washing his stiff shoulders, pressing harder, causing the tension to ebb from them. She washed his upper arms and he couldn't help but flex under the weight of her touch. It was such a man move that he almost groaned at the ridiculousness of it. Kim tugged lightly on him.

"Turn and rinse."

He did and realized he was now facing her, completely nude. Since he was a shifter, he never really had issues with running around buck naked, but he also retained enough of his human side to be modest at the moment.

He watched as Kim's green gaze remained locked on his face.

Maybe she doesn't feel the same pull to me that I feel to her.

"Or maybe," she worked lather up on her hands and moved in to wash his chest, "I'm just trying to be polite and not comment on how you look like you were carved from marble."

Wilson suppressed a smile as he struggled with the fact Kim had indeed read his thoughts. "I'm just happy you picked marble and not carved from a block of cheese."

"Block of cheese?" She scrubbed his chest, seeming to slow her pace as she washed his abs.

"Don't...ask," he bit out as his cock picked then to lengthen at an alarming rate. He'd only just ejaculated. How the hell could his cock be ready to go again?

Kim stepped toward him, seeming unconcerned that water was now covering her as well. She brought her soapy hands to his face and washed him so sweetly that Wilson could do little but close his eyes and savor her gentle touch. She backed away and he tipped his head, letting the water strike the back of his head and rinse the soap from his body.

Kim giggled and the sound went straight to his already excited groin. His cock twitched as he opened his eyes to find her being soaked by the spray of water. The thin hospital gown they'd put her in clung to her, showing off her glorious body. Her dark, rosy nipples showed through, and it took everything in Wilson not to reach out and yank her against him.

She had her eyes closed tight and a hand up, trying to deflect the soapy spray bouncing off him and hitting her in the face. He'd showered with women before. Hell, there wasn't much he hadn't done with a woman, but never had it been like this. For some reason, this was so much more intense than anything he'd experienced before.

Woman, what are you doing to me?

She laughed and peeked out from one eye. "I'm trying to wash the grime off you. Without wearing it all myself." Her gaze dropped to his dick and she gulped, her eyes growing wide. "Umm, uh…" She thrust the bar of soap out to him. "You should probably wash it, erm, *him… umm…*"

Closing his hand around hers, Wilson took the soap from her and inhaled her scent. It did little to alleviate his erection, but he couldn't help himself. "I'll wash *him*."

She nodded weakly before turning and retrieving the shampoo, giving him a fabulous view of her bare backside in the process. He gritted his teeth, cleaning his cock and taking extra time to stroke it while his hands were lathered up.

Not helping here. Flashing that perfect ass at me is a little like shooting me yourself.

Kim stood fast, jerking the bottle of shampoo to her chest. She glanced back at him with something akin to pain in her green eyes. "I wasn't thinking. I just—"

Cursing himself silently for forgetting she could read his thoughts, Wilson shook his head and offered a slight smile. He eyed the bottle of shampoo and her hair. Krauss was right; Kim did have beautiful hair. Hell, she had beautiful everything. "You wash mine and I'll wash yours? Deal?"

She nodded and closed the distance between them. "Okay, but next time we take a shower together, I want candles, romantic music, and wine. Ooo, and bubbles. Understood?"

Wilson admired her ability to joke under pressure. Not many could. "Can I bring my rubber ducky?"

"But of course." She poured a dollop of shampoo into her hands and moved close enough for Wilson to wrap his arms around her.

Unable to help himself. He did just that, wrapping his arms around her and holding her as if they were longtime lovers. Kim didn't complain. No. She stepped closer, leaving his erection grinding against her lower abdomen. She washed his hair slowly, pulling on his head, forcing him to bend slightly so she could reach him completely. The entire event was more erotic, more intimate than anything he'd done before in his long life, yet the act was still innocent at its core.

Taking a deep breath, Wilson stepped backward slightly. He'd burst if he let things advance more. The small space between did little to help alleviate his desire. Kim came with him, closing the gap. He reached up and took hold of her wrists. "Kim."

Don't make me move away from you, please. I'm terrified and you make me forget everything but you.

Her thoughts rushed over him. Watching her closely, he noted her mouth hadn't moved; yet he was positive he'd heard her voice in his head. He wasn't sure what that meant, or why she could read him as well, but he didn't care. He was just happy she was close. He didn't want the moment to end. "Mmm, how about I rinse and return the favor?"

He turned their bodies, planting Kim under the stream of water and then adjusting the temperature so it was warmer for her. She drew in a deep breath, laughing as she clung to him. Bubbles ran off his shoulders and down her body. He wanted to lick every single one of them from her body. She wrinkled her nose as he shook his head, sending water everywhere. Unable to help himself, Wilson walked their bodies back, pressing her against the wall and planting his hands firmly on each side of her head. He bent his head and kissed the tip of her nose. It was quick but enough to let him know he wanted so much more than a peck.

Something pinched the back of his shoulder and he hissed, turning slightly to find a dart protruding from his skin. He kept his body planted in front of Kim's, even though she was still wearing the gown, because he couldn't bear the idea of Krauss's men seeing her wet and in a gown one could see through. He growled as he looked toward the cell bars to see Mendel grinning from ear to ear.

"I told the doc it looks like you're about to fuck her anyways, not to bother with the drugs, but he insisted." Mendel waggled his brows. "Have fun, you two."

"Wil?" Kim leaned around Wilson and spotted the dart. She gasped and pulled the dart free of him. "Ohmygod, what did they—"

Straightaway, it felt as though his skin was burning everywhere at once. The heat moved quickly to his groin. His cock throbbed. The need to plunge it deep in Kim was so great that Wilson had to force himself to step back. "Chain me again."

Her eyes widened. "What? No."

"K-Kim. Chain. Me."

She shook her head and grabbed the sides of his face. Wilson couldn't have fought back even if he'd wanted to. Whatever they'd given him was too powerful. Every fiber of his being wanted to be buried to the hilt in her.

She splayed her hands on his cheeks as her bottom lip trembled. "Why are they doing this to us?"

Because they can, honey.

He couldn't get the words out but knew she heard his thoughts.

Chain me.

She did the furthest thing from chaining him. She kissed him. Slow at first, pressing her full lips to his and then taking it to another level—sliding her tongue out and over his lower lip. Wilson growled, his cock hard enough to hammer nails. As she touched her tongue to his, he lost control, crowding her to the point she had no choice but be pressed to the wall.

The alpha in him demanded he lead the kiss so he did. It was drugging and powerful. He ate at her mouth, and Kim met him every step of the way. He pulled a hand down the length of her body, stopping briefly under the swell of a breast but compelled to move downward more. The thin, soaked gown clung to her, molding perfectly to every curve.

He pushed his thigh between her legs, spreading them. Kim drew in a sharp breath and his mind screamed at him to stop, that she was scared, but his body refused to obey his commands. Wilson slid his hand lower, going for her sex but stopping as he touched her lower abdomen.

A fierce growl tore free of him, and the overwhelming need to protect Kim struck him full force. He caressed her lower stomach, kissing her passionately, and the innate knowledge that she possessed something of *his* came over him. What it was she had, he wasn't sure. The feeling made no sense. Whatever Krauss's men had injected him with was powerful, but the keen awareness Wilson felt as he touched Kim's stomach was even *more* powerful. He quelled the desire to slam Kim against the wall and fuck her until he could move no more and went with kissing her gently instead.

Wilson composed himself and pressed his lips to her forehead. "Let's get you cleaned and fed."

She stared up at him through hooded lashes. "Hmm?"

The fact Kim had gotten lost in their kiss meant more to Wilson than he cared to admit. He smiled and cut it short the moment he felt someone watching them. He kept her shielded from view and glanced over his shoulder to find Krauss standing there, observing their every move.

Fucking pervert.

Krauss looked downright gleeful. "Interesting."

"So you've said," Wilson bit out.

Mendel rushed down the hall and shook his head. "I swear I gave him the dosage you told me to." He put his hands up. "Four times what we gave the other two put together. He should have ripped her apart by now. He should have—"

Krauss lifted a hand, silencing Mendel instantly. He directed his gaze to Wilson. "I didn't think you'd be able to sense *it* in her this early."

It?

Wilson ran the last two weeks through his mind and realized he was still caressing Kim's abdomen. A sick feeling came over him, and he knew better than to think too hard upon it. Kim would read his thoughts, and if what he suspected were true, she wouldn't be happy with the news.

"Have you nothing witty to offer, rat?" Krauss questioned.

Wilson wanted to charge the cell bars in hopes of getting even close to being able to kill Krauss. Kim picked then to place her hand over his as he continued to caress her lower stomach lightly.

Krauss chuckled. "Always so full of smart remarks. Where are they now, Mr. Rousseau? Hmm? Or have we finally found something to silence you with?"

A low grumble began in the back of his throat. He knew he'd growl and attack soon. Kim apparently knew it too because she brought her free hand to his cheek and slid her fingers through his beard.

"Don't, Wil," she whispered.

Krauss snickered. "Listen to the little missus, Mr. Rousseau. She speaks for two now." He paused dramatically. "*You and she*."

Kim tensed and her fear moved over him, taking precedence over the urge to kill Krauss. Wilson directed his gaze back onto her. "I've got you, hon."

"*Hon?* Interesting."

The sound of Krauss's voice set Wilson's jaw on edge. He arched a brow as he smiled at Kim. "If he says 'interesting' one more time, can I kill him?"

She returned his smile and nodded. "But could you hurry? It's getting really cold in here."

Wilson realized the water had turned icy and couldn't help but laugh. Even with cold water rushing over him, he was still horny and still wanted the woman before him. "Honey, I might need to stand under this a while longer. Let's get your hair washed before I realize I'm not a decent guy under all this," he scratched at his beard, "hair."

He sensed Krauss walking away but didn't bother to turn and watch him leave. The news he'd left Wilson with was more than enough to worry about. Having studied and hunted the man with the Immortal Ops, Wilson knew exactly how sick the bastard was, and he knew how desperately Krauss wanted to replicate the I-Ops. Touching Kim's abdomen, Wilson realized Krauss had done the next closest thing to cloning an Op that he could. Wilson also knew he'd die before he'd let Krauss or his men harm Kim or what she carried—a baby.

Chapter Eight

After their shower, food had arrived with a fresh change of clothes for Wilson. Kim had held true and insisted on tasting the food before he had any. She didn't tell him that she drew upon her natural-born gifts to assure it was free from toxins while supposedly tasting it. Kim had watched him eat, at first like he hadn't eaten in months and then slower as he realized she was looking at him. Wilson had then gone out of his way to eat in a civilized fashion, and it broke Kim's heart knowing he'd been through hell, yet was worried about how she perceived him. She'd dropped her plastic fork on the floor, on purpose, and then used her fingers to eat—winking at him as she did.

Her stomach had been touchy and she'd only been able to get a little bit of food in before the threat of it returning on her hit. Wilson had finished the rest of hers as well. He'd practically held her down, assuring she ate at least one more piece of the fruit that had been provided, insisting she needed the vitamins.

When they were finished eating, Kim used her discarded gown and some soap to scrub the area Wilson had been chained to. She hated looking at it and knowing he'd suffered there. It wasn't until he bear-hugged her, pulling her to her feet and into his arms, that she realized she'd been sobbing while she cleaned.

Now that they were ready to turn in for the rest of the night, they were having a standoff over the sleeping arrangements. He seemed to think he belonged on the floor, and she thought otherwise. Though he looked like he might break.

"You sure you don't mind?" asked Wilson.

Kim smiled and shook her head as she put her hand out to Wilson. She'd been trying to convince him to share the gurney, which was doubling as a bed, with her for the greater part of fifteen minutes. The man was so worried about her comfort level that he didn't seem to give any mind to his own. "I'm sure."

"Scoot over and I'll sleep facing the cell door," he said, his voice low.

Staring into his chocolate-brown eyes, Kim did her best to remember to breathe. She'd thought he was good-looking when he'd been covered in dirt and grime. Seeing him clean stole her breath. He was hot. Very hot. "No. I get this side of the bed. They'll think twice about shooting at you with me in the way."

A low growl sounded from him. "You're very stubborn, aren't you?"

"Only when I'm right." She laced her fingers through his and tugged gently. She knew he wasn't like her—he wasn't a full-blooded Fae, but he was something more than human. "Please, Wil. I won't sleep if I'm worried about one of those idiots deciding to use you for target practice again. I'm not asking you to explain how you healed the last shot so fast. I'm just asking that you cut their access to you down a bit."

Something she couldn't read passed over his handsome face before he gave in and climbed onto the gurney. It was cramped and Wilson's muscular body pressed against her. The very hard and very large battering ram he nestled against her lower back made her breathing quicken. She knew all too well just how large he was because of their shower time earlier. Her pulse raced and Wilson purred softly in her ear, nearly pushing Kim over the edge of her self-control.

"I can move to the floor if you're uncomfortable with me being here," he said, draping a large arm over her protectively.

It felt good to be held. Too good to pass up. "No. You're not sleeping on the floor. You've spent the majority of your time here on it. I'll be damned if you spend another second there."

He chuckled. "Yes, ma'am."

Exhaustion began to take its toll on Kim, demanding she relax and sink into the comfort of Wilson's arms. The tension in Wilson's body started to fade away, and for one brief moment she almost forgot about what had been done to her, and that her gut told her Krauss would kill Wilson soon if given the chance. If they didn't get away soon, Wilson would be no more. While she'd only just met him and barely knew him, she cared far more than she should about him. In fact, she cared more about him than any man she'd been with to date. If the sick bastard Krauss got his way, she'd never get to know Wilson more. She'd never know if whatever was budding between them could turn into something more—something real and for good.

Wilson kissed the top of her head and gave her a light squeeze. "Don't cry, hon."

Hon? Cry?

Reaching up, she felt the moisture on her cheeks and realized that she was indeed crying. Did she dare confess what her gut was telling her? That Krauss's use for Wilson was fast running out? "Wil, I'm scared."

"I know. I've got you now. It'll be okay. I won't let them hurt you two, erm, I mean you."

She shook her head, giving in to the urge to confess what was troubling her. "I'm not scared for me, Wil. I'm scared for *you*. He'll kill you soon. I know it deep inside. Please don't ask me to tell you how or why. Just trust me when I say his use for you is drawing to a fast end."

"I know," he said.

She tensed. He knew? "Wil?"

"Shh, hon, don't worry on that just now."

Was he crazy? Why wouldn't she worry about his well-being?

He nuzzled his face against her neck, making her giggle as his whiskers brushed over her neck. "Ticklish?"

"N-no." She tried and failed to suppress her laughter as he rubbed his jaw back and forth. "Stop. I'm serious here. He's going to kill you."

"Yep, probably, but I'll be sure to get you safely out of here first," he said softly.

She tensed. "I'm not leaving without you."

Wilson surprised her by kissing her neck and pulling her tighter against his frame. "Hon, I appreciate your concern. I do, but I'm not worried about me."

She cried harder, and he kissed her neck once more. "Shh, hon, don't cry."

"I don't want you hurt," she confessed. "I want to leave here with you. Not alone."

"Then I promise to do my best to stay alive. How is that?"

She smiled through her tears and nodded, the action making his beard hairs tickle her neck once more. She laughed softly. He purposely rubbed his whiskers against her neck more, and she laughed harder, curling up against him, letting him spoon her as if they'd been lovers forever and this was just another night to them. The thought sobered her instantly, but she didn't want to give up the jovial feeling just yet. "Wil."

"Yes?" he asked, going for her ribs.

She caught his hand and pulled it around, forcing him to hold her. "Tell me about yourself. About how you ended up here, in South America, and here with Krauss. Anything. Just tell me about you."

He was quiet for a moment and Kim thought he might ignore her. "I was in South America on business."

It was the truth but not the whole truth. She didn't press, deciding to let him speak freely. He drew her back against him as he went on.

"It's safe to say Krauss's men caught me with my guard down, and I've been here ever since."

Kim twisted a bit in his arms so she could see his face. "You're being incredibly vague. You do understand that I've bathed you, right? Secrets now seem kind of pointless."

He grinned mischievously. "Yes, but I'd like you to think I'm dark and mysterious."

She snorted.

"So, I'm not pulling off the whole Bond thing?"

She patted his arm gently. "Oh yes. Very well." Laughing, Kim tried to hide her smile, but Wilson grabbed her chin and locked gazes with her. Her breath caught as his lips hovered just above hers. Wanting to be kissed by him way more than she should, Kim pulled herself together and went for a change of subject. "Okay, answer something simple. Like…how old are you?"

He kept his lips close to hers. "How old do I look?"

"Mid to late twenties, but something tells me you're older than that."

He licked his lower lip causing moisture to pool at the apex of her thighs. "It's my wise eyes, isn't it?"

She laughed so hard she snorted. "Oh yes. That must be it."

"I figured as much."

Grinning, Kim laced her fingers through

his. "Thank you."

His brow creased. "For what?"

"For making me feel safe and for making me laugh, Wilson." Kim exhaled deeply and closed her eyes briefly. "I don't even want to think about what it would have been like to wake up without you here with me."

"Bet it would have smelled a right bit better," he said, his lips brushing her cheek.

She laughed. "I can't answer that for fear I'll point out the fact you smelled horrible."

It was Wilson's turn to laugh. He rubbed their joined hands over her abdomen. "So, tell me about yourself. How old are you?"

"How old do I look?" she asked, spinning his questions back at him.

He clucked his tongue against his cheek. "Barely legal, so I'm hoping older than I think."

Kim nodded. "I'll be twenty-six soon."

He didn't look convinced. She smiled. "I swear to you. I'll be twenty-six." She shook her head. "I can't help the fact I look like I just turned eighteen. Sort of a running theme in my family — at least on my dad's side anyway. I'll always look younger than I am."

Way younger.

She kept that thought to herself. It wasn't like she could come right out and tell Wilson that Krauss was right—she was Fae.

Wilson cleared his throat. "So, do you have anyone special back home?"

She locked gazes with him. "Are we counting all men or just the ones who walk on two legs most of the time?"

For a second, he looked nervous. Kim squeezed his hand. "I wouldn't be in this bed with you now if I did, Wil. But I think *Ike* would be jealous if I didn't at least mention him as being important to me since he's the guy I come home to every night. Plus, he shares my room."

"Ike?" Wilson asked, a jealous note in his voice.

Her eyes widened. "Yep. Ike, my pet rat."

Wilson went ramrod stiff. "You have a pet rat?"

"He's very smart and loyal." She stared up at Wilson with a serious look on her face. "They're not dirty animals. I know a lot of people think rats are but they're not. Well, not the domesticated ones, anyways. He comes when you call his name and he's—"

Wilson pressed his lips to hers, ceasing her rambling. His kiss was chaste. He pulled back a bit and smiled. "You don't have to justify having Ike to me, Kim."

"So you don't think I'm weird? My father thinks I am. I rescued Ike from a lab some ten years back and he's—"

"Ten years?" Wilson asked. "Domesticated rats live about three, at best."

That was true, but Ike had bitten her father by accident shortly after she rescued him, and since her father was Fae and immortal, the rat now had a much longer life span. He also had the ability to change colors with his mood, but Kim kept that to herself. Talking about a rat with magikal powers would no doubt make Wilson think she was insane.

"Ike is special."

"Clearly." Wilson's gaze seemed to look straight through her. "He's not the only one."

"You know," she said, deciding to steer the conversation in a different direction. "I think he'll like you. What do you say when we get out of here, you come over and meet Ike?"

"I think I'd like that very much." He closed his eyes and Kim could almost feel how tired he was.

Kim snuggled against him, watching him sleep, knowing it was the first time in a long time he'd allowed himself much-needed rest. She wanted to hate the fact they were thrown together like this, but knew deep inside that she'd have never met Wilson if it weren't for the events playing out as they had.

She lay quietly for a while, wondering about him and what it was he truly did for a living. His vague answers hadn't surprised her. She gave enough of those herself to know how the game was played.

Chapter Nine

Kim came awake to find Wilson crouched before her, snarling at the guards who were on the other side of the cell bars, taunting him. She blinked a few times. Slightly groggy and stunned she'd slept as sound as she had, considering where she was and what was happening. But she'd fallen into one of the deepest sleeps of her life.

Because he made me feel safe.

Reaching out, she let her fingers skim Wilson's shoulder, letting him know she was awake. He didn't face her. Instead, he kept his body positioned in front of hers in a protective manner.

One of the guards laughed. "Loverboy is trying to play the hero."

"Shoot him," the other said.

Mendel pressed closer to the bars, grinning as he held a weapon in his hand. "My pleasure.

Kim pushed off the gurney and put her body before Wilson's. "No!"

Wilson roared and lifted her high in the air before depositing her behind him. He stood tall in front of her. "You won't touch her."

Confused, Kim merely stood behind him, trying to figure out what had set him off to this degree. As Mendel sneered and glanced to the guard nearest him, she got a pretty good idea they'd done something to provoke Wilson.

"What happened?" she asked.

Wilson's head tipped to the side, his shoulders wide and his arms out as if he planned to rip the guards to shreds with his bare hands. It was Mendel who answered as he licked his lower lip. "We were just talking about how we were going to watch your next exam that Krauss gives you. We're hoping you're naked for it."

"Stay the fuck away from her," Wilson said, his voice deeper than normal.

"What are you gonna do, Rat?" Mendel questioned, his lips curving into a sinister smile. "She won't want you after she's had a taste of me."

Tugging on Wilson, she tried and failed to get him to calm down. He was playing into the guards' hands, giving them what they wanted in the way of a reaction. She looked past

Wilson at Mendel. "I will never want you. I'm Wilson's. Not yours."

I'm Wilson's?

Why had she felt the need to say that?

Whatever had prompted it wasn't important because Wilson stopped focusing on the guards and twisted, his attention on her. "Kim?"

As he was partially facing her, Mendel lifted a weapon, pointed and fired at him, not once but twice. Kim screamed, thinking Wilson had been shot with bullets once more. When she grabbed for him and found two darts in his upper shoulder, her eyes widened.

Wilson clutched her, keeping her out of the line of fire of the guards. He took another two darts to the back and began to sway, his eyes closing a moment before snapping open again. His pupils dilated rapidly, and he staggered, stepping back, shaking his head.

Mendel cackled from the safety of the other side of the cell bars. "How do you like the feel of that, Rat? We increased your daily meds."

Horror showed in Wilson's gaze as he

locked gazes with her. "No!"

Kim tried to go to him but he backed up fast, pressing his back to the cell bars. As he did, another of the guards shot him with a taser. Wilson shook and then fell to the floor. Mendel opened the cell door and went right for Wilson, kicking him hard.

"Stop it!" yelled Kim as she tried to go to Wilson but found herself being held back by one of the guards.

The guard lifted her off her feet, and she kicked wildly, trying to break free to check on Wilson. The guard jerked hard around her waist, and she cried out from the pain. Wilson came up and off the floor as if he were on strings. Additional guards poured into the cells, some going for him, some coming for her. One of them pulled a weapon and aimed at her head.

"Give me a reason, asshole," the guard said, his gaze on Wilson.

The minute Wilson spotted the weapon trained on her, he put his hands up signaling surrender. "Don't hurt her."

Mendel laughed. "Paquin, take her to the

cell next to this one."

Wilson's eyes widened. "No. I'll behave. Don't take her away from me. Please."

"I like hearing you beg, Rat," Mendel said, still sneering.

Kim knew Wilson would do something stupid if she didn't calm herself. Taking a deep breath, she tried to temper her breathing and stop panicking. It didn't exactly work, especially when Paquin decided to grab her by the hair and yank her in the direction of the cell door. She lost her footing and fell to one knee. Another of the guards pulled her the rest of the way by her elbow while Paquin dragged her by her hair. The pain caused her eyes to water as she cried out, hitting at the man's hand, trying to get him to let go.

He didn't.

Wilson went nuts. She wasn't sure what was happening in the cell she'd just come from, but it sounded like a war zone. Once she was within the next cell, Paquin released his hold on her hair and shoved her hard. She hit the floor with a thud and gasped.

Paquin backed out of the cell and shut the

door, locking it behind him. Kim rushed to the bars between her cell and the one she'd just been in with Wilson. He had a guard lifted off the floor by the throat. Mendel was there with a different weapon. He took aim.

"No! Don't! Wilson, stop!"

He cocked his head, his gaze coming to her. "Are you hurt?"

"I'm fine. Let the man go. They'll kill you," she said, fear pulsing through her.

"Listen to her, asshole," Mendel offered. "I'd love nothing more than to end you."

Wilson released the guard and stepped back. He gave the guard he'd nearly killed a hard look and the man scrambled away, rushing out of the cell, rubbing his throat. The others followed, locking Wilson in the cell all alone. The guards laughed as they headed off in the other direction.

Wilson came to stand close to her. He put his hand through the bars. "Hon, are you okay?"

She put her cheek to his palm and closed her eyes, leaning her head against the bars. "I'm fine. Please don't give them a reason to kill you."

"They hurt you," he said as if that totally explained his behavior.

"Wil," she said, opening her eyes and locking gazes with him. "I can't watch you die. Do you understand that?"

He ran his thumb over her lower lip. "And I can't watch them hurt you, hon."

She sighed.

He hissed and then backed away from the bars, clawing at the shirt he was in. He ripped it off and bent his head, a sheen of sweat breaking out all over him. It was then Kim realized that whatever they'd had in the darts was causing Wilson issues. He clawed at his chest, making long welts that began to bleed.

"Wil, stop!" she yelled.

"I won't hurt you," he said more to himself than her. "I can't hurt you. Have to protect you."

She wasn't sure how much time had passed before Wilson had worked himself into a frenzy, pacing the cell, mumbling to himself as he shook his head. It broke her heart to see him that way. She wanted to ease his pain, but couldn't.

Paquin returned with additional guards and entered her cell. Wilson was so far gone mentally that he didn't seem to notice them at first. The men grabbed Kim and held her as they laughed at the state Wilson was in.

"Loverboy looks to be having problems with the serum," Paquin said snidely as he held her in the cell adjacent to Wilson's.

Krauss appeared in the hall with a tall, slender, redheaded woman who wore nothing more than a bra and panties. Guards held weapons on Kim and whistled, catching Wilson's attention. He roared and charged the bars between the cells.

"Don't touch her!" he shouted, spittle flying.

"Be a good little boy when they open that cell door, or we'll blow her pretty fucking head off."

Kim jerked against them, unconcerned for herself. All she wanted to do was get to Wilson and assure he was all right. Seeing him struggle against whatever they'd given him was its own form of torture for her. All he'd done since she'd arrived was try to protect her, and she'd not acted quickly enough to do the same for him. She glanced around, surveying their situation, wondering if she could draw upon her natural-born gifts and put an end to this farce. There was a very real chance everything would go wrong and in the end Wilson could be the one hurt unintentionally by her. That was a risk she wasn't willing to take.

The redhead was led into Wilson's cell and the door was closed behind her. She didn't appear to be the least bit nervous. In fact, she looked downright happy to be locked in with Wilson in his current state. For a split second, Kim entertained blasting her with power just to wipe the twisted look of glee from the woman's face.

The redhead undid the front of her bra but it remained closed over her breasts still. "Mmm, come and get me. I'm all yours. They tell me she didn't give it up to you. I will. And you can take me as hard as you need to. I won't break."

Jealousy flared through Kim. She glared

past Wilson at the redhead. "Don't you dare touch him."

The guards holding her laughed. Paquin yanked harder. "Feeling left out? Don't. Doc is having a man brought in for you shortly."

Wilson went ape-shit against the bars, totally ignoring the female locked in with him. He struck the bars, growling, his words inaudible for the time being, his temper flaring. The guards teased and taunted him, laughing as they did, until one stepped too close to the bars and Wilson caught hold of him, yanking him hard. The other guards fought to free their friend from Wilson's grip. The men holding Kim lifted her slightly, jerking her hard, making her gasp as pain went through her at their rough handling.

Wilson released the guard, turning his head in a slow, calculated manner, his gaze on the men holding Kim. "Release her."

The redhead shook her upper body, her breasts bouncing wildly. Wilson never stopped looking at the men holding Kim. It was as if the other woman wasn't even in the cell with him. She didn't take kindly to being dismissed. She grabbed his shirt from the floor and rubbed it over her upper neck, growling, sounding more animal-like than human.

"There," she said, tossing the shirt at Wilson. "I wear your scent. Not her. I can give you what she won't. You know you want it. You know your dick is hard enough to jackhammer through the floor. Use me. Fuck me."

Wilson turned his head slowly, his gaze going to Krauss. "Get your whore out of my cell or I will return her to you in pieces. Don't think I can't smell the corruption on her. She's one of you, and while I don't normally condone hurting women, for her I'll make an exception." He exhaled long and slow. "Return Kim to me or I will bring this place to its knees."

Paquin laughed, tugging harder on Kim. "Because you've been able to do it thus far?"

Wilson didn't bother sparing him a glance. "Before, you had no motivation for me other than my own life. Now, you have Kim. Take her from me and it ends."

Krauss's curiosity seemed to pique. "Are

you saying you'll obey like a good little rat if I permit Kimberly to return to you?"

"Yes," Wilson said with conviction.

"Wil, no," Kim protested. Krauss was crazy and if he knew he had Wilson by using Kim, he'd force the man to do unthinkable things. "Don't give in to them. Don't let them use me to make you mind. Do what you have to do to be free of here."

The redhead approached Wilson, seemingly fearless. She opened the front of her bra, exposing her breasts to him.

Kim's powers tickled her stomach, demanding to be freed. That meant whatever they'd originally given her was wearing off. She narrowed her gaze on the redhead, permitting the slightest bit of her magik to run free. To unleash it fully would mean she'd be forced to act quickly and manage an escape that included both her and Wilson. She wasn't prepared for that. She needed a plan. She needed him on board with it all.

Mostly, she needed to break the truth of what she was to him.

Fae.

The redhead began to choke on nothing but air. She cleared her throat at first, her hand going to her throat. When that didn't work, panic began to show on her face. She coughed more before no sound came from her. She pounded on her chest, racing toward the cell door. The guards there opened it for her and she fell out and onto her knees.

Kim pulled back on her powers, even though she secretly wanted to suffocate the bitch for daring to flaunt herself at Wilson.

The woman gasped, hiccupping in big breaths of air.

Krauss bent near her. "Lividita?"

She panted, fear still in her eyes, giving Kim a sick bit of satisfaction even if short-lived. "I don't know what happened. I think I might be allergic to those new drugs you gave me a little bit ago. I don't feel right. I need to lie down."

Motioning to the guard nearest him, Krauss swept his gaze over the redhead. "If you're allergic to the fertility drugs, you are of no use to me since a successful mating is nearly impossible to obtain without them." He snapped his fingers, no emotion showing on his face. "Kill her."

Lividita shook her head, her breasts bouncing freely about. "No! It's passed. I'm fine. I can do it. I can get him to fuck me. I can."

Krauss laughed mockingly. "For all your assets," he reached out, pinching her nipple, "he paid you no notice. You couldn't entice him even if we had him chained down for you. No. His interests lie more toward the Kimberly persuasion."

Kim licked her lower lip, her mouth suddenly dry. She glanced at Wilson to find him staring hungrily at her.

"Now, let us see if Kimberly has the same willpower as our good Wilson here," Krauss said, snapping his fingers.

The guards dragged a kicking and screaming Lividita off, and when they returned they had a drugged-looking Vic with them. His hands were bound in front of him with handcuffs that looked to be burning his skin. The same as had been the case with Wilson.

"Vic!" yelled Kim, concern for her friend

hitting her hard.

As they unlocked her cell, Wilson went nuts, slamming against the bars. She didn't want Vic hurt by anyone. Not even Wilson.

Without thought, she opened her mouth and blurted, "Wilson! I want him to be the man with me. Please."

Krauss lifted a hand, halting the progress around him. "Kimberly, are you saying you openly accept the fact I want to study the mating habits between yourself and another man?"

"No," she corrected. "I'm saying I openly accept it if that man is Wilson. No other."

"But he controls himself with you," Krauss said slyly.

She met his gaze without fear. "If you're even going to attempt to compare how he is with me versus how he was with Ms. Redhead, I'm going to be sick. I think we both are smart enough to flat out say it. He's not repulsed by me. He may not want to fuck me through the floor but..."

Wilson snarled, and when she glanced at him, she saw all too well that he was willing to do just that.

Krauss mulled it over for what felt like eternity before motioning to his guards. "Leave her."

"Should we return her to his cell?" one asked as another two men carried Vic back down the hall.

"No. For now they can be in separate ones. I need to think on what I've seen and learned today."

Soon, they were gone, leaving Kim alone in her cell and Wilson in his. She went toward him, pressing herself against the bars, wanting to feel his touch. Wilson reacted instantly, his fingers sliding over hers and his forehead coming to the bars.

Nervous, tension-filled tears burst free of her. She trembled, holding on to the bars, his hands over hers.

Chapter Ten

Wilson's chest tightened with each falling tear on Kim's face. The medications they'd injected into him were still pumping fiercely through his system. Even with her fragile state of mind, he wanted to fuck her into oblivion. He hated himself for that.

Focus. She needs you to comfort her, not think about fucking her.

The tiniest of giggles emerged from her. "Actually, I think I might be willing to accept either at the moment. The fucking or the comforting."

Wilson even managed a smile at that one. He bent slightly, lining his lips up with hers. They could only skim because of the bars, but it was enough to help him feel connected to her. "I'm going to get you out of here, hon. I promise."

She fell silent but remained in place. "Do you think they're listening to us?"

"You mean, is the room bugged?"

She nodded.

"No," he replied. "They're jamming any

type of communication device. Keeps others from hearing them and also screws them out of being able to monitor electronically within their own walls."

"So, if I told you something, they wouldn't hear it or know?"

Wilson let his senses ride high, assuring the guards were far from hearing range before he responded. "Correct."

Kim took a deep breath. "The redhead who was here."

"What redhead?" he asked.

"The half-naked lady," she bit out, seeming annoyed. "Let me guess, all you noticed were her breasts."

"Actually, all I noticed was her scent. It was repulsive. Didn't catch her hair color or her breasts. Sorry."

Kim grinned, staying close to the bars. "I did it."

"Did what?"

"Made her choke."

He narrowed his gaze on her.

"Remember the one guard demanding to know about the Fae?"

Wilson nodded. "I also remember you being confused as to what that even was."

"No," she responded. "You recall me *pretending* to be confused."

"Are you telling you're part Fae?" he asked.

"My father is a full-blood and I'm unsure about my mother, but I think she was something magikal too. He doesn't speak of her. Ever."

Allowing the information to sink in, Wilson was quiet. Finally, he locked gazes with her. "Krauss is already aware you carry the blood of the Fae in you. Keep the fact you're aware of it to yourself. If he senses you might be a security threat in any manner, he'll take precautions, and my guess is, separate us by more than just a cell. He won't want to risk us collaborating and escaping." He also knew something else. Something Kim didn't. She was pregnant and he'd be damned if he let her risk herself or the baby. "Promise me now that you won't use any magik. That you'll let me handle this."

"But, Wil, I can help us get out of here. My

powers are getting stronger again. They gave me something that messed with them, but they're coming back."

"No," he said sternly. "I won't risk you, Kim. Swear to me now."

Reluctantly, she nodded. He had a feeling she wasn't planning to obey him.

He pushed his fingers through the bars, taking a section of her hair in his hand. He stroked it gently, inhaling her fresh scent, branding his mind with it, washing away the horrid scent of the other woman.

His cock twitched to life, wanting to be in Kim.

He closed his eyes, remaining in place, knowing this was the greatest form of torture Krauss had come up with yet. Keeping him from Kim.

Time edged by and he could sense the drain on Kim. "Hon, go rest."

"I'm not leaving you," she said sternly.

"Everything on you is stiff and starting to hurt," he replied, hoping she didn't question how he could sense something such as that. While she had confided in him about being

Fae, he wasn't entirely sure she was ready to hear exactly what he was.

Kim released his hand and put her hand through the bars, touching his bare chest, searing his flesh with her fingers. "Actually, I was thinking you're the one with the stiffness problems right now."

She ran her hand downward, trailing a line to his navel and then to the top of his pants. Kim met his gaze, as if wanting permission to go onward.

He caught her wrist gently. "Rest, hon. I'll be fine. The drugs will wear off by morning."

"Wil, let me help you. Please. Don't make me watch them try to have some other random woman take my place." She stared intensely at him. "Please."

Releasing her wrist, he gave a slight nod.

A grin tugged at her lips as she pulled open the fly of his pants. He jerked as her hand found his rock-hard cock there. It sprang out and into the palm of her hand and Kim gasped, trying to close her fingers around it.

"You're huge," she whispered, making male pride swell in him.

She stroked the full length of him, her breath catching again. His cock went through the bars, jutting out and into her cell. At least seven of his ten inches were now on her side. To his amazement, Kim slinked down, putting her head directly in front of his aching cock.

"Kim," he ground out. "You don't have to, ahh…"

She popped the head of his cock into her lush mouth, cutting off his protest. He wanted to instantly explode. Somehow, he held back. She took as much of his shaft as she could with consideration to the bars between them. It didn't matter. It felt divine.

She sucked, her mouth warm and wet. He gripped the bars, groaning as she began swirling her tongue around his shaft as well. He thumped his head against the bars as she bit lightly at the head of his cock. Teasing him.

"Fuck," he sputtered.

Kim stared up at him, a wanton expression on her face. She sucked harder, sliding up and down his cock, adding in her hand to reach the base. The sensation drove him over the edge. Wilson cried out, his balls pulled upward, his cock twitching a warning.

"I can't hold it," he said.

Kim remained in place, her suction on him awe-inspiring.

He exploded, spurting liquid warmth into her mouth and down her throat. She remained in place, sucking him, swallowing everything he was offering her. The sight of her there, licking his cock free of come, was overwhelming.

Reaching through the bars, he tried and failed to touch her face. She was just out of reach. He closed his fingers in midair. "Kim."

Pulling off his cock, she kissed the tip and looked up at him. "Does it hurt less now?"

"Oh gods yes!" He tried to touch her again. This time she moved closer, allowing him to. He caressed her cheek. "Thank you, hon."

"Trust me when I say any time," she replied, surprising him.

Chapter Eleven

Kim pushed her tray of food far from her, refusing to meet Krauss's gaze. The scientist nearest him sighed. "Sir, it's been three days since she's taken any type of food or water. I don't need to tell you the stress this is putting on her system."

Krauss grumbled something under his breath before lifting his hand. "If she eats, return her to the rat's cell."

Wilson, as always, hovered near the bars. "Put her in with me now and I'll make sure she eats."

"And have you attack my guards in the process?" Krauss questioned.

Wilson walked to the back of his cell and put his hands on the wall before going to his knees and then his stomach. He laced his fingers behind his head and spread his legs wide, a sure signal of total surrender.

The door to her cell opened and the guards entered, ushering her out and to Wilson's cell. They practically shoved her in. She stumbled and would have fallen had Wilson not reacted with a speed that shocked her. He was suddenly there, cradling her, pulling her close.

Instantly, her upset stomach felt better and she felt safe.

"I've got you, hon," he whispered, kissing her temple.

She clung to him.

"Get her to eat and to rest, Mr. Rousseau," Krauss said sternly before exiting the hall, taking the guards and scientists with him.

Wilson spun her around and bear-hugged her, lifting her up and off her feet. He covered her face in kisses, making her smile. He walked toward the cot, still holding her off the ground as if she weighed nothing.

"Wil?"

"Shh," he said. "I need to hold you. I need to know you're here and safe with me. Don't ask me to stop or put you down. I couldn't even if I wanted to, and for the record—I don't want to stop."

Relief washed over her. They'd not spoken about her sucking his cock to help alleviate the effects of the drugs he'd been given several days back. She'd never made a habit of doing something so daring with a man she barely knew. In fact, she had only been with two men in her life. The first had been when she was eighteen, and she considered the experience experimental more than anything. It had been too fast to count as much else. The second man she'd given her heart to. Things hadn't worked out as planned with him, and for the longest time she'd assumed he'd been the one for her. She wasn't sure if circumstances were playing havoc with her reasoning and feelings, but since meeting Wilson, she no longer felt she'd let the one for her get away. If anything, she felt like the perfect man for her was now bear-hugging her to the point it was getting hard to draw in air with ease.

"W-Wil." She tapped his shoulder. "Too tight."

He eased his grip slightly before lying with her on the cot, his back facing the cell door.

Chapter Twelve

The sounds of doors opening and closing and footsteps in the hallway alerted her that the guards were doing another check on them. They were like clockwork, every thirty minutes. Wilson generally went on edge whenever they passed, as if he was fully expecting them to do something stupid and shoot him again. With the way they stared at him with hate-filled eyes, she was surprised they hadn't pulled the trigger.

The footsteps stopped just outside the cell, and Kim looked up to see two men in lab coats standing in the mix of guards. One held a clipboard while the other held a file. Kim drew her power up, making all looking in at them believe she was sound asleep.

"How far along is this one?" the man with the clipboard and gray hair asked.

The man with the file scan read it and then stared at the other man. "She's about three weeks."

"Oh, really." The gray-haired man looked impressed. "So this is the female who was instantly receptive?"

She remained still, listening to them as they talked about her.

"Yes. Krauss was so excited her eggs instantly accepted the candidate-in-question's sperm that he thought he'd been foolish in saving the samples for just her. He attempted to inseminate the rest of the supernatural females here, but none of their eggs were amenable."

As their conversation played out in her head, it became very clear what had happened and why she was so valuable to Krauss's project—she was already carrying the next generation of his super-soldiers.

The gray-haired man sighed. "As exciting as this is, I would have liked to see conception take place after a natural mating."

The other man nodded. "I'm guessing Krauss wants the same thing. I have a message from him telling me to abort the child she now carries—without her knowledge, of course—and to call in the observation team. We'll be moving these two to a viewing room and I think he's expecting fireworks."

The gray-haired man glanced at his clipboard. "Has Wilson realized his roommate is expecting?"

"We've told no one outside of the immediate staff, and the meds we've been pumping him full of should block his ability to sense it." He tipped his head. "Though Krauss called me in because he's convinced the rat does know. Says it's what stopped him from giving in to the carnal need to mate aggressively. Something about an inborn knowledge the guy has to protect her and the child she now carries."

A gasp followed. "Are they true mates?"

"I can't even begin to calculate the odds of that." The man shrugged. "I doubt either of them will admit to the signs of being true mates. Besides, how do you test if they can read one another's thoughts or sense when the other is in need? The list goes on from there, none of which we can determine in a lab. The only proof we have will be aborted in about four hours. Shame really, the little bastard would have no doubt been a fascinating hodgepodge. A medical marvel."

They walked off, leaving Kim to soak in all she'd just overheard. She glanced down the length of her body and stopped when she came to Wilson's hand, resting protectively over her lower abdomen.

Oh gods, he knows and it's why he's been so kind to me. He pities me and —

Wilson kissed her neck, proving he was awake. "Mmm, not pity, Kim. Something, but not pity — trust me."

She tensed, unable to remember if she'd spoken out loud or not. Her thoughts went to the promise one of the men had made about aborting the child she'd only just learned she carried. She gasped and twisted to face Wilson. "They're going to kill the baby."

Interesting hodgepodge.

She jerked out of Wilson's hold and fell to the floor. Kim ignored the sting of hitting the concrete and scrambled to her feet. "Hodgepodge? What did he mean?" She touched her stomach tentatively. "It's a baby, right?"

Wilson rose to his feet, looking as if he'd been pulled by strings. He advanced on her, yanking her against his chiseled chest. "Never doubt what you carry. It is most certainly a baby. A baby with special gifts, special abilities, special—"

She gasped. "Wil, I— won't let them hurt —"

He held her tight. "*We* won't let them hurt the baby."

Heat washed up her neck and straight to her face. "Oh gods, Wil, I'm pregnant." She swallowed hard. "This shouldn't be. I take precautions." She blinked. "To the point I'm scary about it. How can they do this to... ohmygod, I don't even know who the father is." She shook her head and buried her face in his chest. "I haven't had sex in months, so it's whoever they—"

"Shhh." He kissed her temple. "We'll get through this. I promise you."

"*We'll?*" She let out a soft laugh. "Just because they did this to me doesn't mean you're responsible."

He tipped her head back, forcing her to meet his gaze. Kim opened her mouth to argue the point more, and Wilson captured her lips with his own. She surrendered to his kiss, needing the comfort he provided. When he was finished, her toes were curling and she was purring lightly, nipping at his jawline.

He led her back to the cot and eased her down on it. For a minute, Kim thought for sure Wilson was going to spread her out and make love to her. When he drew back, she reached for him.

"Get some rest, lil' momma." He waved his hand and Kim could have sworn she felt Fae power around her, comforting her, easing her into a deep sleep.

She wasn't sure how long she'd been asleep when she felt the heat from Wilson's body leave. Opening her eyes, she took a minute to adjust to the darkness and found Wilson near the cell door.

He put his hand against the locked portion. "*Apertus.*"

Hearing him use the Latin word for "open" while he was obviously trying to get the cell door to give caught Kim by surprise. She hadn't sensed the gift of magik in him. From the looks of it, he didn't actually possess it, just the knowledge of how it should work. That or he was new to it all. Either way, it was touching seeing him try. Lifting her hand, Kim let her power rise. She coated the lock with it.

Wilson shook his head and tried once more, repeating himself. This time, the door opened. She stayed in place, watching as he seemed very impressed with himself for having gotten it open. She suppressed a giggle and watched as Wilson slipped into the hall. His entire demeanor changed. No longer did he appear to be the safe, good-humored man she'd lain next to. No. Now, he looked lethal. He disappeared for what felt like forever before creeping back into the cell. He closed the door but didn't latch it. He held two manila folders in his hand.

Kim sat up, no longer caring if he knew she wasn't asleep. "Are those our charts?"

Nodding, he handed Kim's to her and sat.

She opened the chart slowly, half expecting something to leap out and eat her. The past twenty-four hours had been unbelievable. Having a creature charge out at her from an envelope wouldn't surprise her in the least.

Skimming over the first portion of the file, Kim came to a dead stop when she spotted information about the sperm donor. Her eyes widened. There was no way she was reading it right. "This can't be right."

"Why?" Wilson asked, leaning over to peek at the chart.

She pointed at the portion with sperm donor traits listed. "It says he has human, rat DNA, traces of Fae, wolf and panther DNA as well." She shook her head. "This is a joke. This isn't possible. Humans can't be—"

Wilson snatched the chart from her hands and stared at it with wide eyes. "This can't be right."

"Thank you." Kim breathed a sigh of relief. "I'm starting to believe in a lot of freaky stuff. A wererat isn't one of them."

He set her file down and began ripping through his own. "No fucking way!"

"Shhh." Taking hold of Wilson's forearm, Kim did her best to calm him down before all the guards came running. "What is it?"

His gaze locked on her before it slid slowly down the length of her body. "This can't be."

"You said that already."

"I would have known. I mean, I knew you were with child, but I should have known the rest." Wilson let his folder fall to the floor. Files scattered everywhere.

Seeing it was pointless to keep trying to reason with him, Kim went to retrieve the files only to have Wilson beat her to it. "No. Umm, are you tired? You should rest."

She pointed at the cell door. "No. We should get the hell out of here while we can."

"I can't risk dragging you around a jungle, Kim. We'll have to go with plan B."

Kim gave him a pointed stare. "We don't have a plan B. They'll be here soon to abort the baby. I won't let them. I'm leaving now. You need to come with me."

Wilson shoved the folders under the cot portion of the gurney and rushed toward the cell door. He pushed it shut, ran back and practically tackled her. He pulled Kim close and buried her head in his chest. "Someone's coming."

"Oh." Following his lead, Kim pretended to be asleep in his arms. Since her back faced the cell door, she couldn't see who was there but she did hear footsteps. It sounded like more than one set.

"Interesting." The sound of Krauss's hushed voice made her skin crawl. The man had betrayed her in the worst way. "I suspected they may be compatible based on his initial reaction when we introduced her to the facility, but never in my wildest dreams did I suspect they might be mates."

Mates?

"This is the first night since he's been here that he's slept soundly," a voice she recognized as one of the men in lab coats said. "Look at the protective manner in which he holds her. Do you think he senses the truth?"

Krauss chuckled. "No. Parker told me Wilson makes a habit of not thinking. His body is still under the effects of the drugs we gave him. They won't be completely out of his system for a full twenty-one days. So we have a couple of weeks yet. Until then, he'll not be able to notice his scent on her. By that time, he will have worn out his use. I have blood, hair, and tissue samples from him, and you collected enough semen to allow us to freeze a decent amount of sperm. We'll wait until he breeds with her in a controlled setting, re-creating the desired results, of course, then we'll be done with him." He cleared his throat. "Besides, I am rather excited to do an autopsy on him. He is a fascinating creature."

Autopsy?

Kim caressed Wilson's chest ever so slightly. No one would harm him. She would see to that.

"How is it he came to carry the DNA of a rat? I don't remember reading rat as being part of the test list," the other man said.

Rat?

She froze. It couldn't be.

"According to the information Parker gave us, there was an accident at the lab during the days Wilson was there, undergoing treatments to be America's version of a super-soldier. Wilson had been pumped full of the drugs necessary for introducing something new to his makeup, and somehow a test tube from a lab rat was switched with that of a tiger. He was injected and the rest is history. Though,"

Krauss's voice dropped, "I am dying to know how it is he ended up with a blend of Fae, wolf, and panther as well. Parker never mentioned that so I'm thinking he didn't know."

"The child will be one of our greatest successes. Its father is already a mix of supernatural DNA, and its mother carries Fae blood in her. It would also appear they may be natural mates as well. This is almost too good, Krauss. The backers will love this new revelation."

Wilson was the father? And he was a wererat?

She wasn't sure which she should pick to panic about first, so she decided on neither for the time being. It took all Kim had not to reach down and protect her stomach. She wouldn't allow them to harm an innocent child—her child.

"Perhaps we should assure that they are true mates prior to taking this to the backers," Krauss said. "Contact Paquin. Have him sedate Wilson. We'll remove him from the cell and introduce another female to him who is ovulating—not the last female. He had no interest in her. We can introduce another male for Kimberly as well. Perhaps Vic again. He seems most curious as to her whereabouts and unable to control himself when injected with the serum." He let out a twisted laugh. "Perhaps we should chain Wilson and observe him as he watches another male take Kimberly."

"If he is her true mate, he'll kill himself trying to get to her and she'll do the same trying to reach him, Krauss. You've already gotten a pretty good idea of his behavior with the Lividita debacle. Are you willing to risk losing a matched pair? We'll think of another way. But I will say that I think we should attempt to at least separate them. She doesn't need to get used to him being around—not if we're going through with exterminating him."

"Agreed," Krauss said, his voice low. "Send for Paquin. Sedate Wilson and, if need be, use a mild one on Kimberly. If Wilson gives you a hard time, shoot him in the heart. I want his head intact to study. Just hold off on terminating the current pregnancy until we're sure Wilson will be around to plant his seed in her again—this time on his own."

It took all Kim had not to scream, shout, anything to let them know they wouldn't harm a hair on Wilson's head. She decided to go with another approach. She dropped her voice so low it was barely there and whispered, "Swear to me that you won't be afraid of me."

Wilson stiffened. "Kim?"

"Swear it."

"I swear."

"Time for plan B." Kim clutched her abdomen and moaned, pretending to be in pain.

"Kimberly?" Krauss asked, the sound of keys rattling following close. "Get the door open, quickly!"

She rolled off the cot and onto the hard, concrete floor. Her shoulder took the brunt of the impact, but Kim ignored the pain, focusing instead on getting the men into the cell.

The sound of more people approaching left Kim on the verge of panicking. She'd only planned on having to overpower Krauss and the other scientist with him, not guards. It was too late to stop now.

"Kim?" Wilson asked, sounding very convincing. "What's wrong?"

"Sedate him!" Krauss yelled.

Kim peeked out to see the tall, thin man with gray hair headed for Wilson. Two beefy guards moved in behind him. She recognized one of them instantly. He'd been the one who shot Wilson. The man got within a foot of her and she swept her leg out. The large guard went airborne and Wilson was suddenly above her, striking out at the man.

In the blink of an eye, Wilson was in possession of the man's gun and fired at the other guard, taking him down as well. Kim rolled onto her side to find the man she'd kicked lying there with his neck bent at an odd angle. His eyes were wide, unmoving, dead.

Something seized hold of her hair. The next thing she knew, Krauss was there, pressing something sharp to her neck. "One move, Wilson, and I inject her with enough sedative to take down an elephant. She won't survive that. Neither will *your* child."

Kim's gaze went to Wilson. She saw the

hesitation on his face and knew he'd give up his chance to get away for her. That was unacceptable. He tossed the gun aside and put his hands in the air. "Don't hurt her."

Laughing, Krauss tipped her head back farther. "It would appear I was correct in assuming he is your mate. It appears I can control the beast by simply controlling the beast's bitch. Now that he's no longer a threat —"

She glared at him. "I don't know what the hell you're talking about, but know that you won't have to worry about Wil coming after you." She let her power up enough to make her green eyes swirl with white. People had told her it was beyond unnerving to witness. From the look on Krauss's face, they were correct.

He gasped. "What? How? You've never shown any signs of actually being able to wield magik."

Ignoring him, Kim focused instead on the syringe in his hand. She let her magik coat it and Krauss's arm. His hand shook and his eyes widened. She smiled. "Time to administer your meds, Professor."

"No," he said, doing his best to fight back but failing. "Kimberly, think about this. I am offering you the opportunity to make history. To be the Madonna of the Millennium."

Increasing her magik, Kim didn't let up. "What you're offering is to kill the father of the child you saw to it I now carry. And you're offering the chance to let you and your men kill an unborn child all for the sake of science — to see if you can re-create the results naturally." She let her gaze go hard. "No."

"Put the syringe down, Krauss," Wilson said, taking a step toward her.

"I-I can't." Krauss's hand shook and the needle broke her skin. She didn't move. "Do not make me do this, Kimberly. Lift your power. I don't want to harm you."

"I won't live in a cage or allow my son to be born into this. Wil is leaving now." Kim tossed magik at Wilson, coating it with the compulsion for him to leave her behind and never look back.

He shook his head, somehow fighting off her power. "I'm not going anywhere without you. Come with me."

"Your gut instincts told you I'd slow you down. I know that's why you refused to go when we had the chance before." Unshed tears filled her eyes. "Go!"

"Not without you, hon. Not without either of you." His gaze slid down her body. "What Krauss did was wrong, but it doesn't change the fact it's *our* child at risk now. Please don't ask me to leave you or our baby behind."

Guards poured into the hallway and Kim openly sobbed. "Wil, he'll kill you. I can sense it."

Wilson didn't seem to care. "Honey, please don't do this."

The syringe poked farther into her skin. She let her magik loose, no longer bothering to keep a hold on it. It reacted violently to the situation, thrusting Krauss and the syringe far from her. Krauss hit the wall with a thud as she pushed to her feet. Kim planted her body in front of Wilson's a second before a spray of gunfire came at him.

Putting her hands out, Kim directed her power in front of them, catching the bullets in mid-motion. She tipped her head and stared out from swirling eyes at the men who had tried to kill Wilson. As much as she wanted to release the bullets and spray the men with them, she wasn't a natural-born killer.

Wilson's hands slid up and over her own. He pressed his body to hers and put his lips to her ear. "Close your eyes and I'll direct them where they need to go."

She didn't question what he was doing for her, steering her power to eliminate the enemy so she wouldn't have to. She just did as she was instructed. The sound was loud as the bullets sprayed back at their original owners. Kim kept her eyes closed tight.

Wilson had her hand wrapped in his before she could so much as exhale. "Come on, hon. Just follow me. Don't look. Just let me —"

Kim opened her eyes and locked gazes with him. His chocolate gaze made everything seem better. He offered a soft smile. "That's my girl."

They moved through the facility quickly, Wilson holding her hand with one of his and a weapon he'd taken from one of the guards in the other. From the ease with which he handled the weapon, she suspected he was in law enforcement of some sort. Of course, the whole rat DNA thing might mean he was into something even bigger, but she didn't want to think on that at the moment.

He stopped at a closet, punched a hole directly through the wall and then proceeded to unload weapons, handing her two handguns, a knife, and a strap full of grenades. Her eyes widened. "Wil!"

He took the grenades from her and tipped his head, putting them over his neck and through one arm. She watched in awe as he took on a Rambo vibe. She'd seen enough movies to recognize the weapon he grabbed next. It was an AK-47.

"You said you were down here on business." She pointed at the AK-47 in his hand and the grenades over his shoulder. The ones he looked entirely too familiar with for her liking. "What is it, exactly, that you do for a living?"

He arched a brow. "Uh, I'm a postal worker?"

"Wilson."

He grinned. "I kill the bad guys, honey."

"Men like Krauss?" she asked, holding the handguns like they might bite.

Nodding, Wilson took the guns and tucked one into the back of his pants. He held the other, popping the clip and then sliding it back in. He held it out to her. "This is the safety. It's off. Point and shoot at anything that gets close."

"Wil, I can't—"

His gaze landed on her. "Decide now, Kim. It's them or it's us." He ran his hand over her lower abdomen. "I'm not blowing smoke up your ass, honey. I want you and the baby...*our baby*...safe."

"What's a mate?" She needed to know and now seemed like as good as time as any to ask.

Wilson stilled. "You're a supernatural, Kim. What do you know of how other supernaturals marry, reproduce, and all that good stuff?"

She bent her head and averted her gaze. "Not much. My father is tight-lipped about everything outside of the Fae community. I'd heard of shifters, but never actually met any before." She gasped as what he was trying to tell her sank in. "They take a spouse for life—and have one perfect match."

Wilson gave her a tiny nudge and offered a smile. "You okay with this? With, umm, with me? With us?"

A shot whizzed past her head, cutting off her train of thought. Wilson grabbed her and spun her behind him, pointing and shooting with a precision that was both amazing and scary. He grabbed several more weapons, shoving them in varying places—his boots, his pockets, down the front of his pants.

"Vic and Brad are here somewhere," she said. "We have to get them out."

Wilson shook his head. "I heard them moving them yesterday, Kim. I don't know to where. We need to get you out of here and me to my team. My men and I will come back in to free everyone. We can't risk anything happening to you or the baby."

He was right. She nodded.

Kim held tight to his hand as he pulled her through the building, leading her out and past a large home. He rushed toward a jeep and ushered her in, only to realize there were no keys in it. Kim, though shaken from the events unfolding around her, wasn't too far gone that she couldn't help. Putting her hand on the steering wheel, she released her power, starting the jeep instantly.

Wilson leaned over and gave her a chaste kiss on the cheek. "Yep, that's *my* girl."

He gunned the jeep, tearing down a worn path and going deep into the jungle.

Chapter Thirteen

Wilson stared at Kim while she slept. He was afraid to close his eyes for fear Krauss's men would show up and take her from him. No longer did he care about his safety. Now he worried only about Kim and the piece of him she carried.

His mind raced back to the files. The minute he'd read the genetic makeup of the father of Kim's child, he'd known it was him. He didn't even need to get to the name. He had little in the way of clear memories of the weeks prior to Kim's arrival. It was entirely possible, and plainly obvious, that they'd collected semen from him.

He couldn't help but laugh at the irony of not only finding his mate—which he was fast beginning to suspect Kim was—but also knocking her up without having had sex with her.

The rest of the I-Ops would love knowing he'd not been with Kim that way, yet was going to have a family with her.

A family.

Never had he considered settling down and having kids. In fact, seeing his friends mate off, one by one, had sent Wilson into a panic, afraid he'd catch the mating bug. Now that he had a full-blown case of it, he couldn't imagine going back to not having Kim in his life.

The snapping of a twig in the distance alerted Wilson to the fact they were no longer alone. He listened closely, trying to gauge how many of the enemy were there. Whatever Krauss had doped him up with did hamper his normal abilities. Something tickled the back of his mind and for a split second, he could have sworn it was the I-Ops. That was ridiculous. Protocol dictated that even if they had thought he survived the initial attacks, months ago, to only search for him for a certain period of time. That time had passed.

Kim moaned and he went to her side, worried something might be wrong. She jerked awake and grabbed his hand, seeming to calm herself when she found he was with her.

"Get some sleep, hon."

He looked around, sure he sensed someone

near. No part of Wilson wanted to worry Kim or put undue stress on her.

She caressed his hand. "I'm sorry I'm so tired. I used a lot of power to cover our tracks."

"You did what?"

"Don't be mad at me, Wil. I knew they'd hunt us down if I didn't." Her eyelids fluttered, and Wilson knew she was exhausted.

"Kim, how much power did you use?"

"Enough to make them think we went in the other direction and enough to completely cover our tracks in this direction." She released his hand and fear slammed through him.

"No, honey. No!" The idea that Kim could have overexerted herself nearly did what Krauss's men had tried. It nearly broke his spirit. Wilson smoothed Kim's long black hair back from her face and noticed how badly his hand shook. "K-Kim."

She blinked, looking beyond tired. A slow smile spread over her pale face. "I'll be okay. I just need to rest." She yawned. "I think the baby might be draining me a little too. You're worrying so loud that I heard it in my sleep. Stop."

He nodded but had no intention on obeying. "Are you sure you're going to be all right?"

The tiny bit of Fae magik that he carried within him lashed out and ran through her hand. Wilson tried to jerk his hand free of Kim's but couldn't. She turned into him, a smile still on her face, and began resting evenly. He wasn't sure what had happened, but whatever it was, Kim seemed better. Bending, he pressed his lips to her forehead and savored the knowledge she would indeed be okay so long as he could get her out of the jungle and away from Krauss.

Reluctantly, Wilson stood to make his rounds. He didn't want to leave her side. He couldn't shake the feeling that someone was close, but his body was unsure as to whether the person was a threat or not. He patted one of the many weapons he now wore, and it calmed his nerves.

He walked the edges of their campsite, listening closely for anything out of the ordinary. The tickling in the back of his mind happened again, causing Wilson to draw his weapon and crouch, positive something was nearby.

Chapter Fourteen

Kim woke to the smell of food and sat up slowly, her joints aching from having slept the wrong way. She glanced around and found Wilson crouched near a mound of rocks. It took Kim a moment to realize that cooked meat lay upon the rocks. She looked around for signs of a fire but found none.

Wilson turned his head, and as his gaze landed on her, she could see the relief on his face. "You're up. Feeling any better?"

"I am." She pushed to her feet and had him on her in an instant, trying to help. Kim laughed. "Wilson, I'm pregnant, not dying." Kim stilled as the reality of it washed over her. "I'm pregnant."

He touched her cheek. "*We're* pregnant."

Arching a brow, she stared up at him. "Oh really? You planning on squeezing him out in nine months?"

Wilson grinned sheepishly. "If I could, I would. You know, that's the second time you've referred to the baby as a boy. It's too early to tell, isn't it?"

Kim touched her lower abdomen and shrugged. "I don't know. Yes, I guess. Doesn't change the vibe I get when I think about the baby. I just think 'him.' If that makes any sense."

"Makes perfect sense. My friend Melanie can tell the sex of a baby too. She's Fae as well. Might be something to that."

Kim couldn't help but feel a pang of jealousy at the look in Wilson's eyes as he talked about his friend Melanie. She tried to push the feelings away but couldn't. Knowing it was best not to dwell, she opted for a change of subject. "So, where do you call home, Wilson?"

"Virginia. You?"

"Ohio now. Or at least I did. I was—am—attending grad school there. My father and I have lived just about everywhere."

"You're close to your father, I take it."

Kim stared up at the canopy of trees above her and sighed. "Very. We're all we have. I grew up wishing he'd marry again, give me brothers or sisters, but he wouldn't hear of it. Wouldn't even entertain the idea of dating. He seemed to think any women he met would be suspicious as to why he doesn't age, and when the time came for him to move on, to keep his secret, I'd be too attached to them to let them go."

Wilson snorted. "I can relate. So why didn't he just raise you among your own kind…among Fae?"

She stared at him, trying to figure out just how old he was. "I don't know. He has his reasons, I guess. I can't wait to get back and see him, but a part of me is scared to death of what he'll think of me for ending up pregnant."

Wilson scratched his scruffy chin. "That's hardly your fault, Kim. He'll understand. I'll explain it to him and make him understand that I won't let you or the—"

She put her hand up, halting him. "I appreciate that you think you can help, but you can't. He won't accept you into my life. You're not Fae and there is no way my father will be all right with everything." She closed her eyes. "He'll have to accept the baby, but he won't accept you."

"Kim."

"We need to get through the here and now before we worry about what's to come," she said, averting her gaze.

Wilson backed away from her and set about getting her something to eat. He placed cooked meat on an oversized leaf and put some chopped fruit next to it. As he handed it to her, their hands skimmed but he remained silent, alerting Kim to the fact she'd upset him. That hadn't been her intent, but in the end, if they did survive, her father's wrath would be far worse than anything Krauss could do to him. As Kim watched Wilson take his breakfast and sit at the far end of the camp, her chest tightened.

Unsure what to say to make it right, she focused on the food instead. She took a bite of the meat and, much to her surprise, it wasn't too bad. Her stomach gurgled, threatening to react violently if she dared put too much in, so she took it slow. "Thanks for breakfast. I'm a little scared to ask what kind of meat this is."

Wilson didn't respond. He stared at something far off in the distance, blatantly ignoring her. Normally, she would have walked away and allowed the person to act as childish as they wanted, but this was different. She and Wilson had managed to survive something horrific and shared, not only that, but the aftermath of events as well. She still couldn't believe she was pregnant.

He's probably just as shocked he's going to be a father as you are about being a mother.

Her inner voice had a valid point, and it also had a way of making guilt creep up on her. Kim forced a bit of the fruit down before making her way toward Wilson. She held the leaf full of food out to him. "I've eaten as much as I can. Would you like the rest?"

His dark gaze danced over her quickly before he shook his head. "No. I'm fine."

"Wil, talk to me. You're upset and—"

He stuck his bottom jaw out a bit. "Nah, I'm not upset. I'm used to it. I mean, who wants the wererat around any longer than need be? I didn't sign up to be what I am." He slapped his chest. "I signed on thinking I'd be something else."

The raw emotion in his voice stung. Kim did what felt natural. She bent and caught his wrists in her hands. She slid down and sat on his lap, wrapping her arms around his neck. She hugged Wilson tight and rocked him gently. As the tension began to leave his body, she started to hum lightly, needing to make things right with him but not understanding exactly why.

It took a moment for Wilson to warm up enough to hug her back, but when he did, Kim ruffled his shaggy hair. "I think you misunderstood, Wil. This has nothing to do with you being a rat shifter and everything to do with you not being Fae. My father couldn't care less what kind of shifter, if any, you are. Even if you were only human, he'd have issues. I don't know the hows or whys, but I think it has something to do with my mom. I think it's why he hasn't raised me around Fae. My gut says my mother wasn't Fae and that caused backlash with the Fae, and I think my father worries that I'll have an even bigger mark against me if I'm with anyone who isn't full-blooded Fae. Of course, I could be wrong. But that is what my gut says."

He tipped his head and the action left her

lips brushing his. Kim drew in a deep breath as her entire body heated. As their gazes locked, she knew he felt it too. She also knew she was powerless to fight whatever the attraction was between them. "What does your gut say about me?"

"To hold you close and never let you go." She kissed him, and the minute Wilson's tongue dove into her mouth, Kim surrendered herself fully to him. He ran his hands up her sides, coming to a stop just below her breasts. Kim cupped his face, eating at his mouth, needing more than he was giving.

"Uh, Kim," he whispered, tightening his hold on her rib cage.

"Please."

Wilson's gaze softened. "Well, if you insist."

She grinned. "I do."

"Then who am I to argue?" He lifted her off his lap and handed her a gun. "Hold this a minute. I need to unload."

She licked her lips and laughed. "I thought that was the point of me trying to seduce you. You know, so you can unload in me."

It was Wilson's turn to laugh. He chuckled as he pulled a knife from his side. Kim spotted a discarded snakeskin behind him and gasped. "You fed me snake!"

Wilson jolted and caught his hand on the knife. The second she spotted his blood, she felt faint. She pointed at him, not thinking about the fact she still held one of the many weapons he'd taken from Krauss's compound. "You're hurt."

He put his hands up. "Just a scratch, hon."

Shots rang out and it instantly felt as if she'd been punched in the chest. Fire seemed to consume her upper body and time slowed. She glanced down and noticed blood spreading quickly over her shirt. A wave of dizziness washed over her and the next thing Kim knew, Wilson had her pinned to the ground, covering her body with his.

Chapter Fifteen

Wilson's entire body was on high alert. Someone was shooting at them. He glanced around and then down at Kim. "Stay down. I need to... Kim? Kim, honey?"

She stared up at him with wide eyes.

"Kim?"

"Wilson!"

The sound of his name being shouted by a familiar voice grabbed his attention. He turned and couldn't believe his eyes as he found three women standing in a row. Each one was armed to the teeth. "Melanie? Peren? Missy?"

Melanie grinned and rushed toward him. He pushed up and off Kim, still shocked the women were there. His eyes widened as he realized what that meant. "Oh shit, you three went against your mates."

A short raven-haired hottie with the ability to kill just about anything waggled her brows. "We came to get your sorry ass. We missed it."

Melanie nudged her. "Missy."

She rolled her eyes. "Fine, we missed you too."

A medium-height, auburn-haired beauty smiled. "How bad are you hurt?"

He lifted his hand. Still in shock to see his friends had come for him. "Just a scratch."

Missy snorted. "You must bleed like a madman then, unless the blood on you is from the chick who was holding a gun on you."

"What?" he asked, glancing down and noticing for the first time that he was indeed covered in blood.

Peren glanced at Melanie. "I still can't believe you took the shot. I thought it was too far to make, but the moment she pulled a gun on Wilson, I knew you'd do something incredible to save him."

Confused, Wilson shook his head. "No one had a gun on—" He froze. "Kim!"

Turning slowly, he felt his stomach drop as he saw Kim's lifeless, blood-covered body lying on the jungle floor. He rushed to her side, screaming her name the entire way. He did his best to assess the damage, but his mind was spinning with the knowledge he'd left her lying there to greet his friends' wives, all the while she was bleeding to death. "No, honey, no. Talk to me. Kim. Please, Kim."

"Wilson, what's going on?" Peren asked. "Who is she and why did she have a gun on you?"

He lifted his blood-covered hands as hot tears streamed down his face. "She didn't have a gun on me." He closed his eyes tight, hoping it was all a nightmare, that she was really fine. "She was holding *my* gun—*for* me, not on me."

"You three are going to be the death of me," a familiar male voice said. "I swear if this is another wild… You found him?"

"Eadan, hurry," Missy said. "Can you help her?"

A blur of blond moved in next to Wilson. He looked up to find Melanie's brother Eadan kneel beside him, touching Kim's neck, looking for a pulse. When his blue-gray gaze moved upward, Wilson knew it was bad.

He let out an ear-piercing cry before pushing Eadan away from Kim. He pulled her limp body into his arms and rocked her gently. "No! We didn't make it out of there for it to end this way. Kimberly, please look at me. Please, honey."

"Honey?" Eadan asked as he put a hand on Wilson's shoulder. "Who was she?"

"My mate," he whispered, still rocking Kim's body.

The females behind him all gasped.

"Ohmygod no," Melanie said, her voice low. "I didn't know. I thought… Wilson, ohmygod no."

Thunder rolled and wind whipped all around them. At first, Wilson thought it was Melanie's or Eadan's doing since they were Fae. As the heavy press of darkness swept in, he knew better. He also knew that whatever was coming was pissed and headed straight for them. He tried and failed to hold on to Kim's body as the wind ripped him away from her.

He blinked, unsure he was seeing what he was. Hundreds of black birds amassed above Kim's body and instantly formed into the figure of a man who was as big as Green, their largest I-Op. The man's jet-black hair hung just past his ears, and he had a goatee that was cut close. He wore leather pants and a black t-shirt. He looked down at Kim's body and an explosion went off behind him, causing dirt and leaves to go everywhere. He looked up and out from emerald green eyes. "Who harmed her?"

Eadan let out a slew of curses before dropping to one knee and bowing his head. "Lord Culann of the Council. I'm Eadan Daly, son of Medward and Tatianna. We're not the enemy here."

The man put his hand out and over Kim's body. It lifted as if on strings and Wilson tried to charge the man, but Eadan tackled him. "Let go of me!" He struggled against the Fae to no avail. He wasn't at full strength. "Don't touch her! Don't you lay a fucking hand on her."

Melanie and the others were suddenly next to him, yanking on him.

Culann glared at him. "Who are you and what have you done to her?"

"I'm her—"

Eadan elbowed him in the face, silencing him. "He's just trying to protect her, my lord."

Culann put his hand over Kim's chest and hissed. "She's been shot twice. One pierced her heart and the bullets are lead!" He shook his head. "She was here to study plants, not to…" His jaw set and he narrowed his gaze as he moved his hand down more, stopping just above her abdomen. "I will gut the man who dared to touch her! I will—"

Kim's body jerked violently a second before white light engulfed it. Wilson struggled to get to her, but with four people on him, each possessing varying levels of supernatural powers, he wasn't going anywhere until they decided to let him up.

Culann's gaze softened as he stared down at Kim. He swept his hand out and over her once more, and Wilson watched in awe as the blood on her chest vanished. Her eyes opened and she screamed.

"Shh, I am here now. All is well," Culann said, his voice deep.

She looked up at him, appearing confused. "Daddy?"

Daddy?

Her father was some bad-ass council guy? Wilson had half a second to think on that fact before his mind and body told him to go for his mate. He struggled against the people holding him. "Kim!"

She glanced in his direction, appearing slightly disoriented.

Culann touched her cheek. "Is he the man who dared to touch you?"

"N-no. Wilson has never done anything but try to protect me, Daddy. Don't hurt him. Please. He got me away from the men who—"

"Men?" Culann shot magik out, striking a tree and uprooting it from the ground. "I will kill every one of them."

Kim flinched, reaching for her father. "Daddy, please. Listen to me! Wilson stopped them from being able to hurt me. He saved me. He saved the baby."

Culann spun, glaring down at his daughter. Wilson struggled harder against the people holding him. "You were pregnant to start with? By whom?"

"By me," Wilson said, his teeth clenched and his body strained.

Kim, along with everyone else, gasped. She pushed away from her father and ran toward Wilson, putting her body before his. "Daddy, no!" She put her hands up. "Don't kill him.

He's my…" She glanced back at Wilson. "…my mate?"

Culann let out an ear-piercing cry as he shot power out and over the area. "Like hell! My daughter is not mated to a shifter. I will kill him and then you will come home with me."

Eadan, Missy, Peren, and Melanie released him and stood, blocking Culann's path to him. Wilson grabbed for Kim, needing to see she was indeed healed. He looked her over carefully, checking her chest and realizing he was crying as he pulled her close to him. He kissed her temple. "Oh gods, honey, I thought…I thought… Don't ever scare me like that again. We didn't make it past Krauss and his men to have it end like that, Kim."

She wrapped her arms around him and let out a shaky laugh. "I don't know what happened. I was upset you fed me snake, and then it felt like someone hit me in the chest. I woke up to find Daddy…oh no. Daddy."

Kim tried to pull away from him but Wilson refused to let her go. "No. If he wants me dead, fine, but I'll be damned if I let go of you right this second." He ran a hand down her torso and touched her stomach. "The baby? Is he safe?"

She nodded, her gaze going to her father. "It's not what you think, Daddy."

Wilson waved a hand in front of her face. "Kim, I don't give a shit if the man can turn water into wine. I want to know that my son and my mate are okay. Is the baby hurt?"

She touched Wilson's cheek. "He's safe. Daddy saved him." Tears welled in her eyes. "He didn't have to, but he did."

Wilson understood what she was saying. Her father held the power to have saved her life and allowed the baby to die. He didn't. Wilson yanked her into his arms and held her tight before turning his head to look at Culann. "Thank you."

The man glared at him.

Eadan made a move to step forward. "Lord Culann, Wilson is a good, honorable man who would never harm your daughter. He's a member of the I-Ops team and has dedicated his life to protecting those who can't protect themselves."

"Honorable?" Culann asked, his gaze

sinking to Kim's stomach. "So honorable that he plants his seed in my daughter before coming to ask permission for her hand first? Before marrying her? He spent his dirty shifter seed into—"

Kim pushed away from Wilson and pointed at her father. "Daddy, not another word!"

The power in her voice shocked Wilson.

Apparently, from the look on Culann's face, it shocked him too. "Kimberly?"

"No. You will apologize to Wilson this instant. I woke to find myself chained to a bed, after having been a lab rat—" She cringed and stared back at him. "No offense."

"None taken."

She looked at her father. "I woke up pregnant, Daddy. Professor Krauss wasn't who he pretended to be. He's an evil man who wants to make a new generation of genetically altered super-soldiers. He had Wilson chained to the wall." She choked back a sob and Wilson went to her, rubbing her shoulders. "Wilson didn't get a choice. They took sperm from him and implanted it in me. He didn't ask to be a father. He didn't ask for me…and he didn't walk away and leave me to fight my own battle."

Wilson sensed her stress levels rising and rubbed her arms. "Shh, it's okay, Kim. He's welcome to think I'm a piece of shit. I don't care. You need to calm down. You've been through enough already."

She shook her head. "No. It's not okay for my dad to think the father of my child is anything less than what he is — a brave man with a big heart who had a chance at freedom but who refused to leave without me and without his son."

"Stop crying, Melanie," Peren said. "You're leaking power and Krauss's men are combing the area."

Chapter Sixteen

Kim stiffened as the name Melanie rolled from the woman's tongue. She looked over to find a tall blonde woman staring at Wilson and sobbing. Jealousy flared through her. She tried to step away from Wilson's hold, but he refused to let her.

Melanie stared at her. "I'm so sorry. I thought you were trying to hurt him."

Kim wasn't sure why the woman was apologizing and she didn't care.

Melanie swallowed hard. "You're right, you know. The baby is a boy. He's very healthy. Very strong. A survivor." She glanced between Kim and Wilson. "Like his mommy and daddy."

"What the hell is going on here?" a deep voice asked.

Kim looked up to find four men standing in a line. Each dressed as Wilson had been when she first saw him, only they weren't filthy. She took one look at the man in the center, his dark wavy hair tied back at the nape of her neck, and she gasped. "Lukian?"

The man smiled. "Kimberly, what are you doing in South America? Does your father know you're down here?"

A man who had similar features to Lukian's tapped his arm. "Would that be the big scary-lookin' guy who I think might want Wilson dead?"

"Yeah, Roi," a short woman with long black hair said. "That would be the one. He's kind of pissed because Kimberly is pregnant with Wilson's baby."

Lukian blinked and shook his head. "You're what with who?"

Wilson yanked her close to him and kissed the top of her head. "Krauss tricked her and she showed up here, unconscious, about two weeks back. They kept her tied down to a cot, in my cell, just out of my reach." He stiffened. "They took her out each day, talking about monitoring her progress and—"

A hulk of a man with auburn hair growled. "Tell me they did not try to run genetic-altering tests on her!"

Melanie rushed to the man and put her hand on the back of his neck. "Green, shhh.

They did that and so much more to Wilson and her."

A man with amber eyes stared at her and sniffed the air. His eyes widened. "You really are expectin' his baby?"

"Yes, Jon," Wilson said. "She is."

Roi laughed nervously. "I'd make a joke but her father is creepin' me out."

Kim looked at her father. "Daddy, Wilson is guilty of saving my life. That's it."

Her father's jaw locked. "And of saving my grandson's life."

"You're not going to try to make me get rid of the baby?" she asked, tears flowing freely. "Daddy, I thought you'd hate me for what they did. I thought you'd hate the…"

Her father came for her and Wilson eased his grip on her. "I'll handle the men who did this to you. And never would I want harm to come to my family."

He smiled. It looked forced but it was an attempt. "The child you carry is *my* family." He glanced at Wilson. "Are you going to insist on having *him* be a part of the child's life?"

Kim opened her mouth to answer and

stopped. "Uh, umm, we only just broke free of the facility. We've not really talked about what we're going to—"

Wilson took her hand in his. "We're getting married and raising our son."

She gasped. "Wil, I can't marry you. I don't even know you."

"Oh, bullshit, Kim!" he shouted, startling her. "Even if Krauss and his men hadn't interfered, we'd have found our way to one another. It's how these things work, honey. Mates find one another no matter what. What he did to you, to us, is beyond wrong. That does not change the fact it's our baby growing inside you and it certainly does not fucking take away from the fact you are my mate."

"I'm not really your... I mean... I can't be. You're a shifter and I'm Fae. They can't be compatible."

Green let out a long breath. "Actually, every mated pair here will beg to differ. They are all a blend of shifter and Fae matings. I'd like to get you two back to our compound and run some of my own tests." He put his hands up. "Just to be sure you're both okay. Who knows what else Krauss did to you both?"

"Out of the question," her father said. "Kimberly is coming home with me. If that vagabond insisting he's her mate wishes to see her, he can try to come through me."

Wilson charged her father and Kim screamed, rushing between them. "No fighting!"

"Wilson, we need to talk. Tell us everything you can about Krauss and his men. We'll set up a strike." Lukian came forward and stopped just shy of touching Wilson. He smiled. "It's damn good to see your ugly ass again."

Wilson nodded and the next thing Kim knew, the men were all doing very manly versions of hugs. The women cried and clung to Wilson. Much to her surprise, the jealousy she'd felt toward Melanie died down as Melanie hugged Wilson again. Mostly, it had to do with the way Melanie and the man named Green seemed to react to one another. It was easy to see they were in love.

Her father touched her back. "Come, I'll take you home. This is no place for you or the baby to be."

She watched as Wilson continued to hug his friends. "Daddy, I can't leave him."

Her father exhaled rather loudly. "Kimberly, I'm not asking you to never see the vaga—erm, man again. I simply wish to take you and the baby far from harm's way. I think he would wish the same for you and his child."

As Wilson continued to be hugged and held by the people who obviously loved him, Kim nodded. "Okay, but I want you to promise to flash back and protect him. He's weakened from what they've done to him, Daddy. He shouldn't be involved in a strike of any kind."

Lukian pulled Peren into a hug and stared over at Kim. "I agree. It's why, after he's debriefed, he's going home. If he even thinks of lifting a finger to help capture Krauss, I'll shoot him myself."

Kim smiled at her longtime friend. "Wouldn't bother him a bit. Guess they used him as target practice in there at least once a day. Scared the heck out of me when he healed over instantly."

Lukian approached, holding Peren's hand.

He stopped when he was close. "Kimberly, how bad was it for him?"

Her eyes filled with unshed tears as she thought back to the filthy condition she'd found Wilson in. Peren hugged her tight and stroked her back. "Oh, honey, don't even say it. I can see it in your eyes. It was bad. He's safe now." She pulled back. "You're both safe now."

Lukian stared down at Peren. "And that is the only reason I'm not tanning your backside for disobeying my orders and putting not only yourself but our little one in danger too." He touched her abdomen.

Kimberly's father cleared his throat. "So, the rumors are true. The great lycan king mated."

Lukian nodded. "If *only* we could mate off the members of the Fae Council."

Kimberly tuned out their friendly banter and focused on Wilson. The man he'd called Jon hugged him again, and it was easy to see they were close. When they broke apart, Jon did a light, fake punch to Wilson's jaw.

"Nice beard, man."

"And hair," the one called Roi said as he

pushed Wilson's shoulder.

Kimberly stepped closer to her father, needing the comfort of family. "Daddy, I want to go home."

"But I thought you said you couldn't leave him."

Shocked her father was honoring her wishes, Kimberly nodded. "I know, but I'm tired and he's safe…with his friends and family now. We should—"

"If you leave," Peren reached for her, "it will break his heart. They're excited to see him, Kimberly. They thought he was dead and they're like brothers. They really are."

Lukian nodded. "She's right. If you go, Wilson won't be the same."

Kim wanted to agree but couldn't. Wilson seemed healthier and happier having his friends and family near. It eased some of the pressure in her chest she was fast realizing was concern for him. She hugged her old friend and then hugged the woman she assumed was his wife. "Thank you for worrying about him, but he'll be fine. He has all of you back, and though I only just met Wil, I have a pretty good guess he won't take being shut out of the strike against Krauss lying down." Fatigue set in and Kim instantly felt drained. "I'm tired and—"

Her father drew in a sharp breath. "The child pulls on too much of your power, Kimberly."

"I'll be fine, Daddy."

She hoped.

Her father stared at Lukian. "I'll take Kimberly to safety and then return to assist in finding the men responsible for doing this to my daughter."

"Thank you, Culann," Lukian said. "I'd appreciate that. How about I send my wife and her friends with you and Kimberly now? They can help watch over her until we can all," he glanced back at Wilson who was now being bear-hugged by the man called Green, "get back to her."

Kim's gaze went to Melanie, who was watching her closely. She looked away and forced a smile to her face. "I'll be fine, Lukian. Thank you though. Daddy keeps the house warded. Nothing is getting in that he doesn't want there."

Her father put his arm around her. "Come."

She obeyed, refusing to look in Wilson's direction again for fear she'd run to him and never let go. She didn't know the man. Not really. They were strangers thrust together by chance who now had a common thread. One they never planned on.

A baby.

Chapter Seventeen

Wilson tapped the metal table, his mind racing and his body aching to hold Kim. His patience was gone and he wanted to be out there, searching the jungle for Krauss and his men. His breathing was erratic and his pulse was off the charts. Green kept coming at him with a blood pressure cuff and a serious expression on his face. Wilson snarled. "Leave me alone. I'm fine."

"Your test results are saying otherwise," Green said, never missing a beat as he cuffed Wilson's upper arm.

"Yeah, whatever. I want to hunt the bastard down and kill him with my bare hands."

"Because he hurt you?" Green asked, a knowing look on his face.

"Because he hurt Kim!"

Green nodded as if he understood completely before falling silent, taking Wilson's blood pressure. When he was done, he stared down at Wilson. "Without Krauss you wouldn't have a baby on the way right now."

"So you're saying I should send the

bastard a fucking wedding invite?" Frustration churned within him and he puffed a breath of air out slowly.

"No, I'm saying you should calm down, and I was trying to find the silver lining in all of this, Wilson. Kimberly would certainly qualify as one. She seemed very nice and very concerned about you from what Peren tells me."

He huffed. "Yeah, so much so she bolted the first chance she had."

"Wilson." Green squeezed his arm hard. "Peren mentioned something else to me. Something about the drain the baby was putting on Kimberly's system. I think her father took her because he sensed it happening."

Wilson gasped. "I need to go to her."

"What you need," a deep voice said from the doorway, "is to sit and allow that gentleman to continue his tests. If my grandson is going to have his father around, I want to know the man is healthy."

Culann made his way into the room, seeming a little less threatening than the last encounter. Wilson tried to move but Green pinned him in place. "I can and will sedate you."

Wilson rolled his eyes. "Go ahead. I'm used to it."

Culann stared at him. "Are you this difficult with everyone in your life?"

"Is Kim safe?" he asked, ignoring the man's question.

Inclining his head slightly, Culann locked gazes with Wilson. "She is. She's resting. The wards on our home are strong. She's safe. I assure you. I would not be here if she wasn't."

Wilson knew as much. The man was overprotective, but Wilson was damn thankful for that fact. Green finished his newest set of tests and Wilson stood too fast. The blood rushed from his head and he swayed. He would have hit the floor if Green hadn't caught him and eased him back into the chair.

"Oh yeah," Green mused. "You're ready to take on the world. Go lie down, Wilson. I'll get a bag of fluids and we'll work on getting your electrolytes somewhere near normal again. Not to mention your—"

Culann turned as Lukian stepped through the doorway. "Lukian."

Lukian glanced at Wilson. "We've run over everything you've told us and tracked the area where you think Krauss's facility is but found nothing."

Wilson's brow furrowed. How could that be? He'd made a point to keep track of what direction they'd traveled to be sure to come back and strike. It made no sense. "He couldn't have moved the entire facility."

Lukian's gaze bore into him. "Get some rest, Wilson. Maybe you'll remember something later, when you're feeling a little more like yourself."

"Are you saying I gave you bad directions?"

Lukian glanced at Green. "Give him something to help him rest."

Wilson shook his head. "No. I want to find Krauss and then I'm going to get my wife and child."

Culann cleared his throat with a cough. "Until my daughter is claimed, she's no one's wife." He turned to Lukian. "Let's do one more sweep now that I'm here and can lend a hand magikally."

"I'm coming." Wilson tried to stand and crashed to the floor, but this time Green wasn't fast enough to catch him. His head bounced off the unforgiving floor and Wilson's vision blurred. When he collected himself, he groaned and blinked up, his head swimming. "Kim… have to get to Kim. Have to keep her and the baby safe. Have to…Kim."

Culann was suddenly next to him, kneeling down. He put his hand out above Wilson's head. "What you have to do is rest and regain your strength. Until you're healthy, you're of no use to my daughter or my grandson."

Wilson opened his mouth to protest and felt Culann's magik easing over him. He knew what was coming and wasn't strong enough to fight it.

A sleep spell.

Chapter Eighteen

Two and a half months later…

Kim pushed her sunglasses higher as she walked around the shopping plaza. Her father had forbidden her from leaving the safety of their home, but after two and a half months of being cooped up there, she needed to get out. She'd taken to waiting until he was off handling this council affair or that before going for a walk or drive. Today she'd decided to take it one step further and venture out into a crowded place.

She knew from talking to her father that Krauss and a large group of his men had managed to evade capture, and she knew what an asset she was to Krauss. That being said, she refused to live her life in fear. It broke her father's heart and he even tried suggesting they go to Virginia to visit Wilson. She refused. It had taken Kim the greater part of two and half months away from Wilson to realize she'd been falling in love with a man she barely knew. A man who shouldn't be forced to love her for the sake of a child.

Absentmindedly, she ran a hand over the tiniest of swells on her lower abdomen. She was barely showing, to the point she was still able to wear her normal clothing. The doctor, who specialized in supernaturals and worked out of the limelight of public view, assured Kim all was well with the baby.

Kim walked past the food court and the smells turned her stomach. Well, all but one. She glanced around, trying to figure out what seemed to call to her, but found nothing. The plaza was crowded, no doubt due to the fact it was prime tourist season for the area.

Her flat, brown leather dress sandals clicked against the pavement. They had coral beads on them that matched her embroidered voile skirt, which in turn matched the beaded neckline of her v-neck top. Kim had even added bracelets to the mix today. Considering she hadn't felt much like getting out of her pajamas since her return home, that was saying a lot.

She turned back around and bumped into something solid. Heat raced through her body, centering first low in her stomach and then moving lower, between her thighs. She blinked and stared up at a tall man with close-cut brown hair and squared jawline. He was incredibly handsome and every ounce of him looked sculpted. He also seemed to be staring at her with quite the amused yet ravenous look in his chocolate-brown eyes.

"I'm sorry," she whispered, trying to go around him. "I didn't see you there."

He stepped in her path and smiled, clearly trying not to laugh.

Kim's brows knit. "Uh, excuse me, buddy."

He stood his ground. The white shirt he wore showed off his tawny skin, and the faded jeans he had on were snug in all the right places. She especially liked the black combat boots he wore.

Shocked at how rude, yet incredibly breathtaking the man was, Kim gave up and turned around, storming off in the other direction, mumbling under her breath about what a jerk the man had been. She continued on, heading to the other end of the mall. A baby store seemed to call to her. Reluctantly, she headed for it, still uneasy about the entire ordeal.

She stepped over the threshold and felt compelled to head toward the mobiles and other baby toys. Once there, her stomach fluttered and she sensed Fae power. It wasn't hers *per se* but it was close to hers. It was also mixed with something else. Something foreign. The power trickled out and over the mobiles, making them spin, their music playing loudly.

The sales clerk looked over at her and Kim bit her lip, looking away, not wanting to acknowledge what was going on. The buzz of power continued. She backed up, shaking her head, touching her abdomen.

Her cell phone rang and she nearly dumped the contents of her purse in an attempt to get it. When she did, she sounded frantic. "Yes?"

Her father's laugh greeted her. "Something the matter?"

She continued to touch her stomach. "Um, Dad, when Mom was pregnant with me, did I do anything odd? Like wield power before I was even born?"

"Yes. Scared the hell out of her at the start.

We had no way of knowing you'd be that powerful at that age."

Kim looked up at the mobiles, which were still going. Themed bedside lamps began to turn on and off all on their own. The sales clerk went to check on them, appearing puzzled, mumbling about a short in the wiring or something.

"Kimberly?" her father asked. "Is everything all right? Is my grandson making his presence known?"

She was about to say no when a display full of soft, plush balls dumped onto the floor. "Dad, I have to go now." She hung up quickly, touching her stomach once more. "Stop that. It's bad."

A warm chuckle sounded from behind her, making her jump slightly. She spun around to find the sexy man with chocolate eyes staring at her. The minute she tried to walk past him and bumped his arm, the power increased, causing absolute chaos in the store. A baby-blue blanket flew directly at the hunk before her. He caught it with one hand, never taking his eyes from her.

Kim glanced around nervously, noticing everyone beginning to panic. She put her hand on her stomach again and whispered, "No, sweetie. It's scaring people. Stop now."

The power ceased.

Everyone in the store looked around, appearing as if they were on the verge of screaming. Kim assumed the ordeal was over. She was wrong. A package of wall decorations leapt free of a shelf and landed at her feet. They were of cartoon mice, running up and down clocks.

Covering her mouth, she tried not to lose her composure and cry. It didn't work out as planned. She teared up and the good-looking man bent, touching the decorations as if they were fragile and the most precious thing he'd ever come into contact with. He stared up at her with a shocked look upon his handsome face.

Kim rushed past him and out of the store, feeling flushed and queasy. She stopped and went to the side of the mall, pulling her cell out and dialing a number she'd come to know by heart—Lukian's.

He answered on the first ring. "Kimberly."

"Is this a bad time?" she asked, desperately wanting to know if Wilson was all right.

Lukian chuckled and Kim heard Peren's voice in the background. "Hang on a sec, Kimberly. My wife is insisting you come and stay with us. She seems to think you'd bask in the glory of all the pregnancy hormones running around here." He chuckled. "Ouch. Okay, she's now threatening my life if I don't convince you to come."

"Lukian," Kim said softly. "Is Wil okay?"

"Come and you'll know."

She let out a long breath. "I can't come there. I'm trying to figure out a way to cut whatever tie Krauss's experiments did to us. It's not fair to Wil to have that there. He didn't ask for it and I'm sure it's their doing. Not Mother Nature's."

"Kimberly, if you manage to find a way to sever the link between you and Wilson, an update on his condition won't be necessary. He won't survive without you. I mean that literally."

She closed her eyes tight and bent her

head. "Don't say that. He will. He's strong. He'll be fine whenever whatever they did to us is done. I just need to know he's okay. I can't ask my father. He told me if I asked one more time he'd mystically zap me to Wil's side."

Lukian chuckled. "I can see him doing that. Kimberly, I can't update you on Wilson because he's not here. He took much-needed leave."

"I see," she said, glancing up and steeling her resolve. "Good. That's good. He should."

"I gave you his cell number. Hell, I gave you everyone's numbers. Call him."

"I need to go. Tell Peren I said hi and thank her for the invitation. Bye, Lukian."

She hung up and tipped her head against the wall. It took a bit to collect herself but she did. She went instantly to a drink vendor for a bottle of flavored water. Another man approached, this one was only about six foot and had black hair. He smiled and tried to pay the cashier for her water.

"Thanks but no. I've got it."

"I insist," he said, the slightest hint of an accent in his voice. "How often can I say I bought a beautiful woman a drink?"

Trying to be polite, but wanting distance between herself and the man, Kim inclined her head. "As sweet as that is, I'm still going to decline. Thank you though."

"Ah, but I insist."

A muscular arm slid around her waist and a large hand splayed low over her stomach protectively. She gasped as heat rushed through her entire body.

"I think the lady spoke," a deep, familiar voice said. "And I'd really rather another man not buy my wife things, even if it's only water."

Wilson?

Kim's breathing grew shallow as she remained rooted in place, scared to turn around and find it wasn't the man she desperately wanted it to be.

The dark-haired man who had been trying to buy her water put his hands up and nodded. "My mistake."

A powerful arm, much thicker than what she remembered Wilson's being, shot out with money in hand. The man behind her thanked the cashier and then led her from the stand. He pressed his mouth to her ear and she melted against him, closing her eyes and refusing to get her hopes up.

"Are you going to look at me or are you just going to call me a jerk again as you storm off? Or are you going to run away after our son acts up in a store again?"

What?

Kim opened her eyes and looked up to the find the sexy man she'd collided with standing before her. Confused, she took a tiny step back. "Wilson?"

He smiled. "See, I was almost hurt you didn't recognize me. Are you trying to tell me I looked better covered in hair and gods knows what else?"

Kim stared at the man. As she locked gazes with him she knew, deep down inside, that it was Wilson. Granted, it was a much-healthier-looking version of him for sure, but him all the same. Tears broke loose and she tried to look away.

He caught her chin. "Hon, don't cry. I didn't mean to upset you. I'll go. I will but-

but... I had to see you, Kim. I couldn't stay away anymore. I know you said you didn't want to see me but I wanted, no, I *needed* to see you."

She cried harder.

He backed away. "Kim, I'm sorry. I didn't realize you hated me."

"Hate?" she asked, choking on a sob. "Hate? Pfft. I'm bawling because in my mind you've been on death's doorstep since I last saw you. I'm crying because I'm so happy to see you're not only alive but healthy," she let her gaze rake over his incredible body, "really, really healthy."

"So," he dipped his head, "you don't blame me for what happened and for not being able to find and kill Krauss?"

"Blame you?" She stared at him in disbelief. "I could almost hit you right now just for the sheer stupidity of that statement alone. I would too if I didn't know you could kill me with your bare hands."

She winked.

Wilson closed the distance between them, lifting her up and off the ground and hugging her tight. It was then she realized the smell that had caught her attention had been the scent of Wilson—musk, vanilla, and a hint of spice. She wrapped her arms around him, still shocked at how beefy he was.

"Are you normally this…this…" She patted his arms. "Muscular?"

He lifted a brow. "Yes. Why, do you prefer me skin and bones?"

She stared at him, remembering the sight of him when she'd first met him. "Wil, I prefer *you*! *Any* version will do."

He kept her held off the ground. People glanced at them as they walked past, but Wilson paid them no mind. His gaze seemed locked on her. "Mmm, I missed you, Kim. I would have come sooner, but I guess I wasn't as fine as I first thought."

Her chest tightened. "What happened?"

"I'm okay now, don't worry about it."

"Wilson," she said, her tone warning.

He kissed the tip of her nose and smiled. "Funny, I thought things might be awkward between us, but seems to me you've got the scary wife voice down pat."

Kim opened her mouth to argue the point with him, and he picked that moment to kiss her. She pushed against his chest as he inched his tongue into her mouth. Kim moaned, running her hands up his thick neck, over his smooth cheeks, and into his close-cut hair. She ate his mouth and he tipped his head, seeming hungry for even more.

It took Kim a moment to remember they were in a public place. She stopped the kiss and put her forehead to his. "Wil, we, umm, we're in... Wil."

He chuckled. "Yeah, hon, I remembered at the last minute too." He set her down. "What do you say we find somewhere a little more private to talk?"

She took his hand in hers and held tight. The fear of going months between seeing him again hit her hard. "Okay, but promise you'll stay close."

He smiled. "I promise."

Chapter Nineteen

Wilson held Kim's hand, his heart beating madly and his senses on overdrive as he led her to his rental car. He was afraid to speak to her for fear he'd break down. She seemed content just holding his hand as he drove to his hotel room. He parked and led her into the hotel. She kept a tight hold on his hand and pressed in close to him on the way up the elevator. He led her down the hall on the top floor and slid his key card into the door. Once it was open and she was inside, he slammed it shut and yanked her against him.

Every emotion he'd held in for the past two and a half months surfaced. He wanted to be strong in front of her, but it was impossible.

Kim cried and clung to him, shaking in his arms. He kissed the top of her head and lifted her face, staring down at her, uncaring if she saw him crying. She closed her eyes and went to her tiptoes, pressing a chaste kiss to his lips.

"I'm sorry I didn't come and see you," she whispered. "My father tried to convince me to but I couldn't, Wil. I felt like you'd been trapped by what they'd done and I didn't... don't want you to feel forced to be with me."

Unable to believe it, he shook his head slightly and kissed her, not bothering with chaste. When he drew back, her eyelids looked heavy and her lips were parted just a bit. "Woman, from the second I saw you, I knew nothing was going to come between us. If you think for one minute I feel pressured to be with you, think again. I feel pressure to keep from dragging you to the floor and burying myself in you. I feel pressure to keep from hugging you so tight I accidently break you. I feel pressure to keep from telling you things you aren't ready to hear me say...feelings you're not yet ready to know I have for you. That's the pressure I feel."

She cried harder, clinging to him. "I'm so sorry I didn't come."

Wilson didn't tell her it had been for the best. That he'd spent over a month in a drug-induced coma in order to heal the damage Green had feared would be permanent. He didn't tell her that upon waking he'd had to undergo massive amounts of rehabilitation and that he'd used her as his guiding force. He didn't tell her that he fought through it all, beating the odds, plus some, just to be able to go to her and to his unborn child. She wasn't ready to know that—to know he was in love with her.

He held her close and slid a hand down the length of her, coming to rest on her tiny swell of a tummy. He sensed it then, his child in her. Wilson laughed through his tears and Kim drew back, giving him an odd look.

"What's so funny?"

"We're having a baby and we haven't even —"

Her jaw dropped open and she playfully socked his upper arm. "See, I was right. You are a jerk."

Catching her hand with his, Wilson planted a tiny kiss on the back of it and smiled mischievously at her. "I missed you so much."

She blinked, her green eyes seeming more intense now that they were rimmed with red. "I missed you too."

"How are you feeling?" he asked, his gaze sliding to her stomach. "What does the doctor say? Is the baby healthy? Are you healthy?"

"We're both fine." She snorted. "In fact, they tell me your son is measuring bigger than he should be. So, I think we might be having a linebacker or something."

My son.

The sound of that was music to his ears. He reached out for Kim, needing to hold her. She came to him and wrapped her arms around his waist. Her scent filled his head and his cock hardened. He cleared his throat, hoping it would help to clear his hard-on as well.

No such luck.

She slid her fingers into the top of his jeans and clung to him as he kissed the top of her head. She kissed his chest. "I feel like if I let go, you'll disappear. I don't want you to be a dream."

Cupping her chin, he forced her gaze upward. "I'm not. I'm here, and we won't ever be apart again."

She laughed through her tears and he bent, capturing her mouth with his. His kiss was hot and branding. Kim tugged at his shirt, pulling it free of his pants. She moaned into his mouth as she ran her hands over his abs. "I thought you were rock-hard when I helped you shower." She kissed his chest again. "I had no clue you were normally like this. You're quite the intimidating specimen of a man."

He smiled. "Who is still," he took her hand and pressed her palm against the distended flesh in his pants, "rock-hard."

Kim licked her lower lip and fire shot through his body. "Mmm, I see that. Hard. Very hard."

"Kim," he whispered. "I want to throw you onto that bed and bury myself so deep in you that we forget everything but the moment."

She blinked and stared up at him with lust-filled green eyes. "Then by all means, get the show started. I'm dying here, Wil. Touch me."

He groaned, his cock twitching. "I can't. *We* can't. I don't want to hurt the baby."

Laughing softly, she touched his cheek. "Sweetie, you won't. Please give this to me. I need to feel you in me. I need to know you're really here. That this isn't a dream."

"It's no dream, and as much as I want to take you and claim you fully as mine, I want to do things right."

She appeared puzzled. "Meaning?"

He smiled as a knock sounded on the hotel room door. "Wait right here."

Chapter Twenty

Kim waited in her spot as Wilson disappeared from her line of sight. She heard him talking softly with someone and then he reappeared with a long garment bag in his hands and a huge, sexy smile upon his handsome face.

"Wil, what's going on?"

He set the garment bag on the bed and turned to face her. "I planned a weekend for us, Kim. I want us to get to know one another the way we should have without outside interference."

A swell of emotions rushed over her and she nodded, wiping her cheeks in an attempt to keep them tear free. "I-I'd like that very much."

He exhaled looking relieved. "Don't worry about your father. He knows about this. He's the one who told me where you'd be today."

She gasped. "I didn't think he knew when I left the house."

Wilson chuckled. "Oh, he knows. I don't think he'll ever not have some sort of mystical tab thing going on you. Though he swore to me that he'd stop while we're together. I don't blame him one bit."

Kim rushed Wilson, tossing her arms around him and hugging him tight. He lifted her off her feet and laughed as he spun her around. "You're an amazing man."

He set her down and blew on his knuckles, arching a brow cockily and smirking. "Yeah. I know."

"Dork," she said, slapping his arm lightly.

He caught her around the waist and made her pulse speed. "Yeah, but I'm your dork. Don't forget that."

Kim ran her thumb over his lower lip. "And here I thought I'd want a pony when I grew up."

"Well," he blushed, "we have to take the good with the bad."

"And are you bad, Wil?" she asked, hoping he was the bad boy she sensed he could be.

He winked. "I'm an angel, honey."

She stepped out of his hold and stared upward.

"What are you doing?"

"Waiting for God to strike you down for lying." As her gaze met his, Kim had to fight with all her being to keep from peeling her clothing off and begging Wilson to take her.

Wilson motioned to the garment bag. "Yours is in there. I'll step into the other room and change into mine."

"Huh?"

He pointed to the bed. "Open it and see."

She did and her breath caught. A long, pale green evening dress with a scalloped-edged bottom lay there. It looked to be sleeveless and form-fitting. That wasn't all. It was a Vera Wang. "Ohmygod, Wil, it's beautiful!"

"It will bring out the green in your eyes," he said, lifting it and handing it to her. "When I saw it, I knew it was the one I wanted you to wear tonight."

She shook her head. "I can't accept this. It's too much."

He gave her a funny look. "No it's not. It's not nearly enough."

"Wil," she said sternly.

He wrinkled his nose and laughed as he rushed out of the room. "Get changed, woman, or I'll do it for you!"

Kim held the dress up and was shocked to see how accurate his guess on her size was. Wilson was turning out to be a man of many layers. She hoped he'd allow her to see all of them.

She dressed quickly and found a pair of matching heels near the closet door. They were exactly her size. Kim slipped them on and waited for Wilson to emerge, nervous about how she looked. She skimmed her hand over her lower abdomen, which seemed to show more with the way the dress hung. It was easy to see she was pregnant in the gown. She sighed and felt the weight of someone's stare on her.

Turning, she found Wilson standing in the doorway. He was dressed in a tux that looked stunning on him. He was also staring at her with an off expression on his face.

Kim went to move away but he was there in an instant, spinning her in a slow circle, staring at her as if he wanted to devour her.

I look like a whale.

He shook his head. "No, honey, you look

like the most beautiful woman in the world. The mother of my son." He put his palm on the swell of her stomach and closed his eyes. "I know we didn't plan on this, but I'm damn happy about him…" He slid his hand up her body slowly. "About you, Kim. About us."

Kim groaned and pinched his ass. It was hard to get enough flesh to do so, but she finally managed. "Pretend like that hurt, bucko."

Wilson had the courtesy to act as if she'd wounded him with her pinch. He took her hand in his and led her from the room. Kim wanted to ask where they were going, but the thrill of the surprise kept her silent.

He led her onto the elevator, putting his hand on the small of her back and staying close to her. The doors opened on the second floor and the view left her speechless. The hotel corridor was lined with white roses. Red rose petals covered the floor and Wilson offered a half smile as he drew her out into the hall. "Ready?"

"Wil?"

He glanced sheepishly around. "Do you

like it?"

Kim gawked at her surroundings. "You did this? For me?"

Nodding, he put her arm through his and continued down the hall. She stepped on the soft petals and followed close by his side. They went past all the doors on the floor and headed straight for a staircase. Wilson tightened his hold on her arm as he led her down the stairs. A large sign spanned the top of the archway that read "The Cellar." Confused, she glanced at Wilson only to find his game face was on.

"Wil?"

"This way," he said, stepping through the archway.

Kim stared around in shock. The cellar was anything but a basement. It was more like a trendy underground restaurant. It had a domed shape, and tables lined the sides of it. Much to her surprise, the entire restaurant looked to be empty.

Wilson grinned as he bent and kissed her cheek. "I figured we were under the watch of enough eyes when we first met. This, here and now, will be just the two of us." He shrugged as a waiter approached. "Well, and him, but that's all."

"You bought the place out for the night?"

"Do you like it?" he asked, sounding hopeful.

She waited until they were seated and the waiter had gone off to get her glass of water and Wilson's wine before commenting. "This is all too much. It's wonderful, don't get me wrong, but none of this was necessary. Just getting to see you again was enough."

Reaching across the table, he took her hand in his. "I want you to have everything your heart desires."

She stared around and then at him. "This is nice, but I don't expect or want this all the time. If you think I'm this high maintenance, then you really don't know me at all."

"But your father is a member of the—"

Knowing where he was headed with this, Kim put her hand up and stopped him. "Wil, just because I'm the daughter of a rich and powerful man doesn't mean I was raised with a silver spoon in my mouth. Is this what you like? Are you this high maintenance?"

He snorted. "Uh, no. I just sort of go with the flow most of the time."

She rubbed her fingers over the back of his hand. "What do you do for fun?"

"We should change the subject," he said, looking nervous.

Kim nodded, sensing the reason he didn't want to talk about it. "You're one of those guys. The kind who spends his free time romancing women."

"I *was* one of those guys, Kim. I'm not now and I haven't been that way in over six months." He took a sip of water, looking warm. "How about you? What do you do for fun?"

Deciding to allow him to change the subject for now, she tipped her head. "As of late I seem to sit around in my pajamas crying nonstop." She forced a smile to her face. "But I used to like to read anything I could get my hands on, I love to study plants and love anything to do with science, I like to run, swim, anything really."

He grinned. "Great, it's painfully clear I need to get used to the fact you're smarter than me."

She knew he was joking, and she also sensed he was a hell of a lot smarter than he let on.

The waiter approached and inclined his head, speaking in French.

Much to Kim's surprise, Wilson answered, taking a moment to ask her what she wanted and what she didn't think would make her stomach upset. She selected a light pasta dish and apple juice. When Wilson relayed her order, the waiter arched a brow at the apple juice.

She blushed. "I can't help that I crave apple juice almost all the time."

Wilson put his hand over hers. "Nothing wrong with that. I'm betting it's a hell of a lot better for the baby than other things you could be craving."

The waiter left them, and Kim tried and failed to stop staring at Wilson.

He smiled. "Something wrong?"

"I just can't believe you're here and you're safe and well."

"I did promise to meet Ike, so I thought it

best to hold up to that commitment," he said with a twinkle in his brown eyes.

Covering her face, Kim realized why he'd been so open to the idea of her pet rat. She laughed. "Wow. Ike really will be jealous of you. But," she peeked out at him, "can you change colors with your mood? Ike can."

"You have a mood rat?" Wilson flashed a bad boy smile. "Woman, you were so meant to be mine."

She blushed and reached out, taking his hand in hers. "This is nice, Wil. Having you here."

Chapter Twenty-One

Wilson choked back the emotions rising in his throat. Gods, Kim was even more beautiful than he'd remembered. He'd actually been in town for close to three days now, watching her from afar, unsure of the reception she would give him. He'd been unable to hold back anymore when she was at the mall. It was entirely too cute when she'd run into him and not recognized him. He didn't expect she would. He was surprised when she turned down the obvious advances of the other man. The guy was good-looking and seemed like the type of guy girls like Kim would go for. He was also the type of guy Wilson wanted to throttle for daring to try to be with his woman.

My woman.

He smiled at the knowledge she was indeed his mate. Even her father agreed. It had taken a while to win over Culann, but Wilson was persistent if he was anything. Culann had even proved himself to be a valuable ally during the planning of the weekend Wilson had in store for Kim.

Absently, he slid his free hand over his right jacket pocket, touching the small box there. He wanted the woman before him to be his wife in every way possible—human, Fae, and shifter.

Kim tipped her head slightly, her green eyes soaking him in. "It's strange, don't you think?"

"What's strange?"

"The way I feel about you when we really don't know each other. Is it the mate thing? I've asked my father about it and he filled in some blanks, but since he's not a shifter, he's not entirely sure how this all works." She closed her eyes a moment. "He just knows I care about you deeply." When she looked up at him again, her expression said she more than cared.

Wilson lifted their joined hands and planted a kiss on the back of hers. He wanted to tell her that he cared for her too—that he loved her despite the short amount of time they'd been together. That wasn't what fell out. "Yes, the mating energy between us is kind of all-consuming. It's nature's way of assuring the reproduction of our species continues. Lust times ten," he said with a nervous laugh.

Kim stiffened and pulled her hand free of his. "Lust," she repeated, seeming to stew on the word.

He cringed, knowing he'd opened his mouth and inserted his foot. "Kim, I…"

The waiter arrived with their food, and Kim went out of her way to focus on her plate, not him. Shoving his foot in his mouth was a syndrome he'd suffered from all his life. It was hardly new. That being said, he hoped the evening would go over without a hitch. That he'd give his mate a romantic evening she'd never forget.

*

Kim stabbed at her food, still mulling over Wilson's use of the word "lust." He continued to stare at her and she ignored him, forcing her focus to the food before her, rather than the hunky man. It was hard.

Her tummy fluttered and she stopped and put a hand on it, knowing the baby was sensing her stress. She exhaled slowly. "I promise not to stab Daddy," she said in a soft voice.

Wilson chuckled and touched her other hand. "What if Daddy lets you stab him? Would that make you smile again?"

Unable to help herself, she grinned. "Maybe."

"Kim," he said, touching her cheek. "I'm a little nervous about freaking you out."

"What do you mean?"

I mean that I feel a hell of a lot more for you than lust, woman.

His voice echoed in her head, and she narrowed her gaze on him, his lips having never moved. Her chest was tight and her eyes moist as his words hit home. Nodding, she had to swallow several times before she could speak.

"I feel that way too." She cleared her throat. "More than lust, that is."

Wilson lifted her fork and took over feeding her as if she were a child. Though he managed to make it sexy. As her lips eased around the fork, Wilson moaned. She laughed and touched his wrist, leaning closer to him.

Dinner went the rest of the way without any more hiccups, and she couldn't remember a time when she'd laughed more. Wilson was naturally funny, to the point she had to beg him to stop for fear she'd be sick from laughing so much.

The walk back to the hotel room was as magikal as the dinner. Wilson held her hand, his gaze remaining almost entirely locked upon her all the way to the room. Kim wrapped her arms around his neck and tugged, forcing him to bend a bit so she could kiss him. He did and their lips met. She closed her eyes and savored the taste of him. His tongue slid around hers artfully and her body heated.

"Mmm, Kim," he said softly against her lips. "We're stopping here long enough for me to grab something, and then I have more planned. Do you need a wrap for outside? Will you be chilly?"

He opened the door to the room and eased her in gently.

She tugged on him, jerking him against her. "Stop avoiding being close to me."

"I have to," he confessed. "If I don't, I'll end up buried in you."

She smiled. "I know."

"Kim."

"Wil."

He grunted. "I want to do this right. I want to make everything perfect."

"If you don't hurry up and give me what I want, I will hit you with so much magik you too will change color with your mood."

*

He lifted her gently and walked her toward the bed. Kim laughed and ran her hands over his chest. Wilson laid her out on the bed and savored the sight of her spread out before him. Kim tugged down the top of her dress, revealing her ample breasts to him. Her nipples were slightly darker than he remembered, and he wondered if it had something to do with the baby.

He bent, taking one of her pert nipples into his mouth while he caught the other between his thumb and forefinger. Kim moaned and arched her back to him. He sucked gently, his cock throbbing to be free of his dress pants and buried in her. He switched, sucking on the other nipple. Kim melted under his touch and ground her hips up against him.

"Wilson, please."

A sly smile covered his lips as he kissed a line down her belly. When he reached her lower stomach, he found the start of a swell. His child grew within her. The thought made him soar. Wilson fumbled with her dress, trying to figure out how to free her from it before surrendering and hiking it up and over her hips. It was bunched at her waist, revealing a tiny brown thong. Kim reached to try to undo the dress but Wilson liked seeing her like that —partially undone and ready for him.

He caught her wrists and planted his face into her thong-covered mound. The scent of her arousal made him growl with pleasure as he nudged the material aside with his chin. Releasing her wrists, he set his attention on her sweet pussy. A tiny thatch of black hair covered the mound and the rest was clean-shaven. He spread her folds and inhaled deeply, never wanting the moment to end.

Pressing his face into her wet cleft, Wilson growled and licked a line down her. Kim jerked and rubbed her body against his face. He flicked his tongue over her clit, pleased at how responsive she was to him. Each swipe of his tongue made her body arch and her breath catch. He thrust a finger into her, surprised at just how tight she was. Her pussy clenched his finger as she moaned. He began thrusting it in and out, gently at first, easing her channel open little by little. He licked her clit, moving his face back and forth, stimulating her body more and more.

Kim opened her legs wide and then clamped them together on the sides of his head, holding him in place as her orgasm crashed over her. Wilson laughed into her pussy, lapping up her cream, proud to have given her pleasure. When she finally released her hold on his head, he stood slowly, staring down at her gorgeous body. "Woman, you need to be very aware of the fact that I'm going to spend eternity fucking you."

"I'd be happy if you spent the next hour

doing it. I want you in me so bad, Wil."

Grinning, he undressed, tossing articles of clothing haphazardly around the room. He crawled up and over her, his body skimming hers. Never had being above a woman felt so right. So meant to be.

"Spread your legs for me, hon," he said, kissing her lips softly.

She obeyed.

He pushed into her, slow at first, her pussy gripping him. His jaw went slack at the tightness of her cunt. He gritted his teeth, every muscle in his body straining with the urge to ram into her. To pummel her until he spent his seed in her.

He refrained, wanting to savor the experience for as long as he could.

So perfect.

So wet.

So warm.

So welcoming.

Kim slipped her arms around his neck, drawing his head downward, her mouth capturing his. He lost himself in the moment, unable to restrain himself from taking her like a depraved man any longer. He drilled into her, a long, slow hiss coming from him as her cunt grasped at his cock, demanding it stay buried deep within her womb.

"Wilson," Kim whispered, a cross between a moan and a cry. "Yes. There. Right there."

His gums burned and pain flashed through them. He had only a second to think upon what would cause his mouth to shift before instincts took over and he slammed his mouth down upon the tender flesh of her exposed breast. He bit at the same second his cock jetted seed out and into her. As his shaft filled her with the proof of his release, her blood filled his mouth. He swallowed down the rich, coppery fluid before drawing his mouth from her bosom. He licked the wound, the healing agents in his saliva acting quickly.

Staring down at her through the eyes of a predator, he panted, still locked deep in her. "Mine."

Kim's eyes were closed and pleasure was a wash over her face. She nodded. "Yes. Yours."

Power slammed into him, catching him off guard. When Kim gasped, he realized it happened to her as well. The walls of her pussy responded, quivering around his cock as she came. She stared up at him, shock evident.

The tiniest of threads seemed to weave between them, linking them more, cementing their shared bond.

His claim.

Making her officially his mate.

His shoulders heaved as he took deep breaths.

"Are you hyperventilating now that I'm really your wife?" she asked, a half-assed grin at the ready. "Way to get the cold feet a hair too late."

"Oh, hon," he whispered, kissing her passionately. "It's not that. I'm the happiest man alive right now."

"Then what is it?"

"My body feels like it's going to rip apart."

She winked. "You ripped me apart in the best way possible. You should do it again. Now."

He would have, but he was serious. Something was wrong. His back pinched and his arms felt as if they were on fire. Panting, he rolled off Kim and went to his feet, raking his hands over his face.

Lifting his hands, he noticed them shaking oddly. He put one out and the picture on the hotel wall burst into flames. He rushed for the bathroom and water. Kim sat up, reached out suddenly and the fire died away. She looked at him and arched a brow.

"We're going to need to work on your ability to wield magik before you burn the place down."

He blinked. "I did that?"

"Yep. Looks like you're a little like Ike. When he bit my dad, he picked up Fae traits. Since you already had some and you're a supernatural…"

It hit Wilson then. "I now have more Fae traits."

"Yes, baby, you do. And you're clearly a danger until we get you trained."

He smiled wide. "Will you carry a whip? Please say yes."

She tipped to the side and tossed a pillow at him. "Oy."

Chapter Twenty-Two

Wilson stared at the monitor, his hand locked with Kim's as Green continued with the ultrasound. "He *is* a big boy. Her doctor is right," Green said.

"He's healthy, right?" Wilson questioned, his emotions threatening to run free on him.

Kim winked up at him, all smiles. "Of course he's healthy. Green, what about the other tests you ran? The ones to check his genetic makeup?"

"He still worrying nonstop if the little guy carries the DNA of a rat?" Green asked Kim, totally ignoring Wilson.

"Hey, I'm allowed to worry. The last thing I want to do is pass on—"

Kim sat up as much as she could, given the fact she was nearly five months pregnant. "Everything about you that I absolutely adore?"

He opened his mouth to protest.

Green shook his head. "A wise man would shut up now."

"You're not saying Wilson is a wise man,

are you?" Jon asked, entering the exam room.

"Look who is here," Kim said, patting her stomach. "It's your godfather."

Wilson grinned at his friend. "Look," he said, pointing to the screen. "That's my boy."

"Our boy," Kim corrected.

"Yes, *our* boy."

She took a deep breath. "What about Krauss and his goons? What if they come for the baby?"

Wilson kissed her temple. "Let us worry about Krauss, hon. You just worry about keeping our son from destroying department stores again. And worry about keeping your dad from skinning me alive when I tell him I want at least three more boys, okay?"

"Three more boys?" Kim gulped. "My father is the least you have to worry about, bucko. I'm likely to skin you myself before then."

THE END

Tactical Magik (Immortal Ops Series)

Book Five in the Immortal Ops Series.

Eadan Daly has thrown himself into the role of the sixth Immortal Ops team member, even though it wasn't supposed to be a permanent position, and has forged a brotherhood of sorts with the other men. When he's asked to go on a solo mission for the Paranormal Security and Intelligence Branch—PSI, for short—he's not so sure he wants his old job back.

Inara Nash is a survivor, doing what she must to get by. On the run for years from an organization she doesn't fully understand, she tries to stay under the radar. When a blond hunk arrives and claims he's her savior, she suspects her luck might have finally run out. Sure, he's hot and looks like he'd be good in bed, but there is something almost magikal about him that defies reality. And if there is one thing she's learned during her life in the paranormal underground, it's that you never trust a magik.

Excerpt from Tactical Magik (Immortal Ops Book Five)

Chapter One

Present Day. Location: Classified.

"I said I was sorry," Geoffroi "Roi" Majors stated as he glanced back at Eadan from the front passenger seat of the Hum-V. The vehicle that currently held five not-so-small guys was hardly inconspicuous. It was also less than comfortable. They stuck out like sore thumbs, and Eadan Daly had to question the wisdom of this being their getaway vehicle. This one wasn't reinforced to help stop bullets. It seemed a lot like tissue paper at the moment. Pretty much all it had going for it was cool factor. One that screamed government or paramilitary group. A blinking sign on the top would only make it worse.

Shoot here. There is a better-than-average chance you'll hit your target.

With the entrance Lukian had been forced to make to get to them, they might as well have sent out engraved invitations to the enemy to come shoot at them there. Would have proven as effective.

"This thing go any faster?" Wilson asked, fidgeting in his seat.

Lukian didn't comment. He merely glanced at the rearview mirror. His glare was enough of a response.

Eadan's ears were still ringing from the hail of gunfire around them. Had he not assisted with his magik, they'd be picking lead out of his ass.

Out of all their asses.

He'd expended more power than he should have, but it was required. Unfortunately, he'd be feeling the ill effects of that much usage for probably a week or more. Unless he met up with a hottie at a bar and spent the night rockin' her world. Sexual energy would speed his ability to rebuild his natural-born power base.

He looked to his left at his fellow Immortal Ops (I-Ops) teammates, Jon and Wilson. Jon shook his head, indicating they should not accept *this* apology from Roi either. They'd been steadily rejecting Roi's attempts to make amends for the past twenty minutes.

Wilson tapped his fingers on the doorframe, an annoyed breath easing from his lips. "You left without us. In a hostile zone, mind you. Might as well have painted a damn target on us yourself."

"No," Roi protested, twisting in the seat. His dark hair fell partially onto his face. "I told you already I thought Lukian was getting you. And, see, he got you."

Lukian, the team captain, snorted as he drove. He tended to be on the quiet side yet always managed to get his point across. Eadan had been unsure how to read him at first but was learning more and more each day.

"What?" Roi grunted and tossed his hands in the air. "Fine. I wasn't listening during the briefing because I was exhausted."

Green's voice came over their comms unit earpieces. "Stop worrying. Your wife and your girls will be fine."

Roi shifted around in his seat as he tapped his wrist and spoke into his comms piece. "You're the one who told me it's uncommon for a woman pregnant with twins to go to term. That means I could become a father any day now. I'm not ready yet. I only just got the nursery finished. I haven't set up college funds for them yet. I didn't…"

Roi was going to spiral out of control again. He'd been doing that more and more of late. Seemed as if the prospect of fatherhood was going to do what the enemy couldn't—kill him.

Lukian reached over as he continued to drive and touched Roi's arm. "Relax, brother. There is plenty of time for all that."

"Why am I the only one freaking out? Your wife is due soon too," Roi said, sounding frantic.

Eadan held back a groan. All this talk of pregnancies was getting on his last damn nerve.

Green's chuckle echoed through their earpieces. He was currently tucked away in a tiny location the team had preselected as base during their current mission. Green was their eyes and ears on everything else going on, a technical guru who also happened to be the best at patching them up when need be.

"Peren has another two months. Missy, with the twins, probably won't go that long. Melanie has two and half months left and Kim has—"

Wilson leaned forward. "Just under five months left."

Eadan nudged Jon. "Is it just me or have our missions deteriorated into recipe swaps and what-to-expect-when-your-mate-is-expecting moments?"

"No," Jon said, his eyes widening. He looked almost scared, as if he too might catch the bug to discuss upcoming babies. "It's not just you."

"I'm fairly sure we were once feared," Eadan added with a laugh. "Now we're the labor patrol. We make the enemy shake in their boots—well, right after we're done talking about the first signs of contractions."

Wilson shook his head. "No. Not feared. Misunderstood. We were totally misunderstood. And just wait, you two will see what this is like when you meet your mates. Then we'll all laugh at you."

"No," Eadan said. "You'll give us burping

tricks to help the kid with gas."

Visit www.MandyRoth.com for more information. Also, be sure to check out the spin-off series in the Immortal Ops World, PSI-Ops, Shadow Agents, Immortal Outcasts and Crimson Ops.

Dear Reader

Did you enjoy this title and want to know more about Mandy M. Roth, her pen names and all the titles she has available for purchase (over 100)?

About Mandy:

New York Times & *USA TODAY* Bestselling Author Mandy M. Roth is a self-proclaimed Goonie, loves 80s music and movies and wishes leg warmers would come back into fashion. She also thinks the movie The Breakfast Club should be mandatory viewing for...okay, everyone. When she's not dancing around her office to the sounds of the 80s or writing books, she can be found designing book covers for New York publishers, small presses, and indie authors.

Learn More:

To learn more about Mandy and her pen names, please visit http://www.mandyroth.com

For latest news about Mandy's newest releases and sales subscribe to her newsletter

To join Mandy's Facebook Reader Group: The Roth Heads, please visit

https://www.facebook.com/groups/MandyRothReaders/

Review this title:

Please let others know if you enjoyed this title. Consider leaving an honest review on the vendor site in which you purchased this title. Reviews help to spread the word and boost overall sales. This means more books in the series you love.

Thank you!

CPSIA information can be obtained
at www.ICGtesting.com
Printed in the USA
LVHW111630280620
659220LV00004B/712